TERRITORY: PREQUEL

By

Susan A. Bliler

Copyright © 2012 by Susan Bliler

www.susanbliler.com

ACKNOWLEDGMENTS

Thanks so much to Sandara
for the awesome cover art.

Check out her work at:
http://www.sandara.net/

Special thanks to Cindy Bliler
for cover layout and formatting.

DEDICATION

For Mama
Our true pack leader

Chapter 1

What in the fuck is he doing here? Chloe seethed at the sheer audacity, her dark almond shaped eyes glinting with fury. Releasing her mother's hand, she stood and stepped out of the pew before she strode determinedly down the aisle without looking back.

Outside the church, she found a secluded corner and tucked her slight frame into the dark recess before exhaling slowly. Her breath escaped in a great white puff. The rain had been falling for five straight days, and in Montana cold always accompanied the rain.

Chloe tilted her head up to the drearily darkened sky and let the fat drops splash down on her too warm cheeks. *Five days of rain,* and five days since her brother had been killed. God she wished she smoked, or drank, or had some horrible habit that could give her even a minimal respite from the throbbing ache of misery that had settled in her chest. She couldn't breathe and she didn't want to. She wanted to find a dark corner, curl up, and sleep for a hundred years so that when she woke the memory of her older brother would have faded and she wouldn't know the dull pain that now squeezed her heart so tight that she didn't think she could stand it.

How much pain can a person take? She'd asked herself that question over a hundred times in the past five days. *God, I can't do this!*

Tears stung at the back of her eyes and she inhaled deeply, surprised that her tears would choose now to come forth. All throughout the day she'd waited for her tears, but they hadn't come. They hadn't come when her mother moaned in agony as her brother's casket was wheeled into the church, and they hadn't come when she'd stood to tell the room full of strangers what a wonderful human being her brother had been. Finally, after enduring dry-eyed the misery of her only sibling's funeral, she'd concluded that she'd cried every last tear that she could and there simply weren't any left within her to shed. But now tears welled in her eyes and it disgusted her that her emotions were so raw that she honestly didn't know if they came from sadness at the loss of her brother or anger at the appearance of her enemy.

Pushing off the wall, she dropped her head and looked down at her hands. They were small hands, but capable. Anger roiled within her as she envisioned stalking back into the church and wrapping those very hands around the throat of Dell Blackbird. *Motherfucker! He's got some serious brass to show his face here!* It was insulting. As if her family hadn't been injured enough by the Blackbirds, now in their most solemn hour Dell had the nerve to show up.

For what? Out of respect? Her teeth clenched and her hands balled into tight fists at the thought of Dell extending his hand to her mother and offering up his sympathies. *Son of a bitch!*

But even the anger couldn't last. She was too exhausted. Over the past five days she'd run the gamut of her emotions, and she'd felt pure raw sentiment more powerfully than she'd ever believed she could feel. Now it seemed she couldn't hold on to any one emotion longer than a few fleeting moments. It took too much energy, and at the end of the day she knew that no amount of anger or agony would bring her brother back.

***

Dell walked confidently to the front of the church. His powerful frame donned the appropriate form fitting black suit. He shouldn't be here he knew, but it wasn't in his character to stay away. He heard audible gasps as members of the Lott family watched him stalk to the front of the church.

The room reeked of pain and sadness. It was stifling, but the worst was the heavy air of regret. Not his own regret, but God knew his contributed. Then slowly, the deeper he walked into the church, the scent of anger grew stronger as more and more acknowledged his presence. It was a risk to be here, but it was honorable and whether the Lott family knew it or not, he was an honorable man. His family was honorable.

He pulled a braid of sweetgrass from the inside breast pocket of his dark suit jacket and stepped up to the casket. Donnie Lott looked more peaceful in death than he ever had in life. Dell had only ever seen the other man angry and he swallowed back bitterness at the knowledge that the Blackbird family had been the cause of Donnie's anger and death.

Donnie was a mere two years older than Dell, the exact age of Dell's older brother, Mace. Staring down at the still cold form, Dell remembered the ridiculous headline in the local paper four days earlier. 'Two Men Fight to the Death Over Suicide of Local Woman.'

Dell exhaled deeply as he tucked the sweetgrass under Donnie's stiff fingers. "Swift travel brother." He turned then and was slammed by the overwhelming scent of blinding fury. His eyes slid over the church, not making direct eye contact with anyone in particular as he tried to pinpoint the source. When a slender female in the first row stood and turned to storm down the aisle, he knew the scent had come from her. *Chloe.*

Dell had heard nothing but good things about Donnie's sister. While he'd never actually met her, he knew that she was well liked in the community for her generosity and kindness.

Dell watched as she shoved open the back doors of the church and disappeared into the rainy night. With her fury gone, the room settled back into their pain and misery and none was more prominent than that of the elderly woman in the front row.

Solemnly, Dell approached the woman he knew to be Donnie and Chloe's mother. If she knew who he was, Bea didn't let on as she stood to accept his outstretched hand and to thank him for coming. Dell inhaled deeply trying to catch the slightest hint of anger or resentment, but there was only pain. It was the type of pain that could only emanate from a mother attending the funeral of her only son. He'd scented the same agony yesterday when his family held ceremony and his mother watched as his own brother was buried.

"On behalf of my family, I'd like to express to your our deepest regret and most sympathetic condolences. Please know that we pray only peace, hope, and strength for you and your daughter."

The frail looking woman clasped Dell's large hand in both of hers before nodding and looking up. Her mournful brown eyes shimmered with unshed tears, "I too pray we *all* find peace."

Her words spoke volumes. She knew who he was, and with a divine beauty, she stood before him wishing him and his family well as she stood attending her own son's funeral. Dell's throat thickened with emotion as he nodded once before lifting her hands to his lips and kissing them before he released her soft fingers. Dell made no eye contact with any other attendee as he strode from the church.

***

Chloe tucked her body tighter into the dark corner as she heard the church doors creak open. *Is it over?*

She groaned inwardly as she realized the funeral continued, someone had just decided to leave early. She eased out of her dark recess and inched down the wall to peer around the corner that hid her from view of the church's front steps. Catching sight of the hard frame dressed in a sharp black suit, she recoiled instantly forcing her frame harder against the wall. *Dell.* Anger swelled within her again as she debated confronting him. But what was the use? It wouldn't solve anything.

They killed your brother! She shoved off the wall, prepared to confront a man she'd never even met, but her resolve dissipated when the sound of approaching footsteps had her plastering herself back up against the wall.

"Well?"

Chloe heard the female's voice and peered around the corner to see that Dell was standing face to face with an unknown woman, his back to Chloe. Like Dell, the woman had raven black hair, but hers was pulled up into a tight chignon that emphasized high cheek bones.

"How'd it go?" The woman prompted.

Dell sighed heavily before offering a weary sounding, "As good as could be expected."

"No problems?" The woman prompted.

Problems? Why would there be problems at a funeral? Granted the Blackbirds weren't welcome, but it's not like Chloe's family would cause a mutiny at their arrival. Well, no one besides her.

Chloe moved her head trying to catch a better glimpse of the woman who stood only shoulder high to Dell even in her black high heels. The woman was dressed for attendance, her outfit nearly replicating Chloe's. Both women wore black pencil skirts with black suit jackets, but while the other woman's perfectly applied make-up and well done hair were shielded from the downpour by the black umbrella she held, Chloe felt like a drowned rat. Her hair was now plastered to her head, and she could feel the rain running down her face in chilly rivulets. She didn't care; she knew she wasn't going back into the church.

"No problems." Dell conceded.

Chloe thought she caught him motioning with his head in her direction, so she quickly pulled back and quietly settled herself back into her dark corner. *Does he know I'm here? Impossible!* She tried to listen in on the rest of Dell and the woman's conversation, but the rain picked up and the cacophony of rain splatter on asphalt and nearby passing cars drowned out their words.

Chloe tilted her face up and closed her eyes, letting the rain pelt down on her face. *I don't give a fuck! Rain. RAIN!* she challenged mocking the skies.

Distracted only momentarily by Dell and his friend, Chloe's thoughts reverted to her brother. The heavy weight of sorrow that she'd been carrying for five straight days settled back onto her chest. She toed off her heels and completely ignored them, leaving them on the ground next to the wall as she pushed off it and began walking away from the church, no longer caring if Dell or his friend spotted her.

She was halfway down the block when the sharp cadence of heels clicking rapidly down the pavement caught up with her.

"Chloe."

She ignored the call.

"CHLOE!"

She didn't turn to acknowledge the woman that had been talking with Dell even as she caught up to Chloe and lightly touched her arm.

Instead of trying to stop her, the woman kept pace as she switched the hand in which she held her umbrella in an effort to afford some sanctuary to Chloe as well as herself.

"I'm Cindy."

Chloe didn't break her stride as she gritted her teeth. *Like that should mean something to me!*

The woman continued, "Cindy Gorr."

"And?" Chloe bit out angrily, wanting to be alone.

The woman grabbed Chloe's arm roughly and jerked her to a stop. "My maiden name is Blackbird. I'm Mace's sister."

Chloe stuttered to a halt and turned on Cindy with angry eyes. "What do you want?" She could see now that the woman had a light sprinkling of freckles high on her cheeks, but that was the only interruption to perfect tan skin that left no question as to the woman's native ancestry.

"Dell would like a word."

Chloe snorted. "No. That's a word, take that to him."

Cindy's features darkened, "You can come willingly, or I can make you."

"Well," Chloe scoffed, "you can certainly fucking try."

Cindy frowned at the slightly taller woman, "It wouldn't be a fair fight."

"If you find yourself in a fair fight," Chloe began, "then you haven't planned properly."

Cindy's frown cracked into a genuine grin. She too enjoyed the expression and used it often. She tilted her head studying

Chloe silently, deciding that had they met under different

circumstances, the two would have been fast friends. But they

hadn't, and Chloe had no idea who or what she was fucking with.

"He won't wait much longer."

Chloe shook her stiff fingers before she ran them down her

rain drenched face. "Look, I just buried my brother." Chloe

cocked her head, a scowl marring her features. "You remember

him? Donnie. Donnie Lott." Chloe took a step closer in

challenge, "You know, the one *your* brother killed."

"You aren't the only one to have suffered the loss of a

much loved brother."

Chloe shook with rage as she balled her small hands into

tight fists. She'd never wanted to punch someone so bad in her

whole life. Instead, she dipped her head and ground out through

clenched teeth, "*My* brother was fighting to protect what was his.

What was *your* brother doing?" Chloe watched as Cindy took a

calming breath.

"I don't expect you to understand. Look, I'm not here to fight with you. Dell just wanted to have a word with you and I thought it'd be better if..."

"If what? I don't want to talk to him." Chloe pointed in the direction of the church. "I don't want to talk to *you*! What I want is for you people to leave me and my family the fuck alone." Chloe turned on Cindy and strode angrily away.

Unable and unwilling to do anything else, Cindy merely watched until Chloe was swallowed up by the blackness of the October Montana night.

***

As Cindy shook off her umbrella and slid into the car, Dell didn't have to ask what happened. He'd heard it all.

Dell turned to stare out the window and the light that shone down the church steps in multi-colored patterns as it filtered through the intricate stained glass.

"You should let it go brother."

Dell turned to stare at his sister. "Our brother killed hers because our brother's wolf claimed the man's wife!" His tone was angry. "How can I let it go Cindy? We've ruined their lives and we can't even explain to them why."

Cindy shook her head, "It's not Mace's fault his wolf claimed a married woman. He couldn't control it, you know that."

Dell's eyes glittered with rage. "You're wrong! Mace's *wolf* couldn't control it. But it's the man's job to control the wolf." Dell shook his head as his eyes slid down to his hands, "This never should have happened. Three people are dead because Mace couldn't control himself. Because of what he was…of what we are."

Cindy argued, "He was in love Dell! Do you get that? He was madly and deeply in love with a woman he couldn't have. He got that. It was his wolf that didn't understand, but it wasn't his fault. Do you think Mace knew that woman would kill herself over her inability to choose between him and Donnie?"

"No," Dell barked, "but if Mace had stayed away, let the man grieve for his wife in peace none of this would have happened. They'd both still be alive. Donnie and Mace would both still be alive."

Cindy turned to stare out her own window, "You don't know what it's like Dell. When you find your mate you'll know, but right now, you have no idea what it's like to have your mate. To *claim* your mate. I couldn't imagine if another woman had a claim to my Mike. If I couldn't have him." Cindy sobered turning and reaching out to touch her brother's knee, "I can honestly tell you I probably wouldn't have done anything differently than Mace had."

Dell's features contorted into a sneer, "It's inexcusable. And it's weak."

Cindy's lips twitched into a rueful smile as she reclined back into the buttery softness of the leather interior that lined the vehicle. "You'll see big brother. One day, you'll see."

"I don't want to see. I want to make amends with that damn family for what we've done, for what Mace has done."

"There's nothing you can do Dell. They don't want our help or our apologies. What would you say to her anyway? 'Hi, my name is Dell Blackbird. My brother killed yours but it wasn't his fault. You see we're shifters and my brother's wolf claimed your sister-in-law. So you can see the only resolution was for your brother and mine to fight to the death over love of the same woman.'" Cindy threw up her hands, "Christ Dell, let it go. I'm telling you if we don't walk away now, this is only going to end badly."

Dell shook his head. "I can't let it go. Did you scent her rage? She hates us." He shook his head, his eyes drifting back to the rain, "Unchecked rage begets action. We don't need enemies. We can't afford them. I *will* fix this—for their sake and for ours. I'll make it right."

"You can't bring them back."

Dell reached up to rap the window with one knuckle. "I know, but I can't just leave things as they are. That family, that girl...she deserves an answer."

Cindy sighed, "And *that* is the one thing you can't give them."

Silence hung between them for several moments before Cindy sighed and added, "And she's hardly a *girl* Dell. She's the same age as you."

Chapter 2

Chloe stood in her mother's bathroom drying her long black hair with a fluffy white towel when she heard the front door click open then close just as softly. Draping the towel around her shoulders, she sucked in a breath, bracing her hands on the sink as she met her own gaze in the mirror.

She looked like hell, and for her mother's sake, she wished she didn't. There was nothing she could do about the dark circles under her eyes, so she picked up a brush and attempted to tame her long straight locks into some semblance of order. She opened the cabinet and retrieved her mother's lipstick. Applying a thin layer to her full lips, she took a deep breath then descended the stairs.

"Hi mom." Chloe wrapped her arms around her mother's slight shoulders from behind. She felt her mother stiffen then her shoulders hunched and a long moan of agony tore loose as her mother's body wracked with uncontrollable sobs. Chloe knew she'd fought hard to hang on to her misery through the service, but now alone in their own home; her mother had no strength left.

Chloe didn't speak, she didn't have to. She knew there were no words that would offer her mother any solace, so she did the only thing she could. She simply held her mother as her heart broke into a thousand little pieces within her chest, as her own warm tears slid silently down her cheeks.

***

Hidden by the thick foliage of the woodlands behind the two-story brick house, Dell watched solemnly as Chloe held her mother.

He noted how the younger woman fought to keep from breaking. Her lip trembled and she seemed angered by the tears that slid free. But even outside, in the thundering rain yards from the house, he still caught the scent of the anguish within. The scent so mirrored his own mothers torment that it clenched his belly into one giant knot.

He hated this, all of it! Every single second of suffering that had occurred in the past two months had been the direct result of his family's lineage. He gritted his teeth and seethed at the weakness: Donnie's weakness at not being able to control and keep his woman; Beverly's weakness in not being able to deny Mace; and Mace's weakness at not being able to walk away from Beverly.

Mama and Cindy had warned Dell, Mace, and their younger brother, Briggs, that once they found their true mate that they'd be unable to deny her regardless of circumstance. Now, Dell growled at the injustice of it all. He didn't want to be bound to someone in such a manner. It wasn't fair, and the current circumstances proved that it wasn't right.

Never before had he questioned what he was…until now. Today he wondered if his family, his kind, weren't simply beasts after all.

***

Chloe loosened her grip on her mother, bending to brush her lips against her mother's temple. "Come on mom. Let me make you some coffee."

The older woman shook her head, "I just want to lie down."

Chloe followed as her mother headed for the stairs.

"Most have gone to the reception, but if any guests come," Bea halted briefly, "feed them and thank them."

Chloe nodded wordlessly. Her mother could always rely on her to do as asked. At twenty-seven, it wasn't a matter of obedience, rather a matter of respect.

Once her mother disappeared at the top of the stairs, Chloe busied herself picking up her mother's home.

Bea's typically immaculate home was now cluttered with dirty dishes, wads of dirty clothes, and piles of yet-to-be discarded newspapers from the past several days. It was a testament to her mother's suffering. Even when their father had passed, her mother's home had remained spotless. But now, eyeing her surroundings, Chloe could almost feel her mother's release on the tight reins of control she had clutched so fiercely. It was terrifying. The prospect of her mother succumbing to her misery was a despair that Chloe knew she'd never overcome. Chloe bit her lip worriedly, *How do I keep mom from going under?*

When the doorbell chimed, Chloe raised her eyes to the ceiling hoping her mother wasn't disturbed by the noise. As she strode quickly to the front door, she smoothed her hands over her hair and stopped with her hand on the knob to suck in a reassuring breath. *Should it hurt this bad just to breathe?*

Chloe opened the door without bothering to paste on a pleasant or non-committed welcoming smile. Instead, she opted for resigned tolerance, which was exactly what she felt. She didn't want visitors and her mother didn't either, but it was how her community offered condolences.

Pulling the door open, she sucked in another agonized breath as her eyes locked on Dell Blackbird.

He stood in her doorway, drenched, his head lowered as rain dripped from his lithe frame. He was wearing the same suit he'd worn to the funeral, only now instead of looking sophisticated and controlled, he seemed dangerous. The lines of his body were taught...rigid. It was startling, and Chloe realized she should have been frightened, but she was too damn mad to be frightened.

Her brows knitted in anger as Dell lifted his head, his eyes locking with hers.

When Dell growled fiercely and fell to the floor, Chloe wasn't quite sure what was happening. A wave of nausea crashed over her, followed immediately by a peaceful serenity. It was the first time she'd felt at peace since her brother's death. The emotion drew a whimper from her parted lips even as her knees threatened to buckle.

She braced her arms in the doorframe, clutching the wood tightly until she regained her composure. When Dell hissed out a long agonized breath, Chloe instinctively bent to offer aid before she quickly righted herself.

With one hand clamped on her fluttering belly, she mustered up as much hatred as she could. "No need to bow to me dog!" She fought to keep the confusion from her tone, but she knew she failed miserably.

Dell's head snapped up, his strong features contorted in fury and pain. One hand clutched his belly while he growled through gritted teeth, "I am no dog!"

Chloe sneered down at him. She'd heard the stories. It was a small town after all, and everyone knew the story. Blackbirds were supposedly descendants of skin walkers, shape shifters, wolves. It was a joke at first, but over the years the rumor had garnered the Blackbird family first mockery, then respect, and then fear. Now the town's folk regarded them with what Chloe could only compare to some semblance of reverence.

"You're all dogs. Filthy beasts." She lowered her head to deepen her sneer. She hated him, and she wanted him to hurt like she was hurting. "Someone should put you down."

Dell struggled to his feet, drawing in a ragged breath. "Keep it up and I'll show you how beastly I can be."

Chloe's sneer faltered and she flushed angrily at the telling catch in her voice, "You already have."

"CHLOE!"

Chloe's head snapped round to discover her mother frowning disapprovingly at her daughter from the top of the stairs. She eyed her mother for several tense moments and when she turned back to Dell, he was gone.

"*That* was uncalled for," her mother admonished.

Chloe ignored her mother's comment as she gulped in several breaths of fresh air. Her belly felt queasy and her muscles shook as they fought to keep her upright.

"What did you do to that young man?"

Chloe's frown eased into innocence, "Nothing." She turned then to eye her mother, "I didn't touch him he just...fell."

"You know who he was?" her mother accused.

Closing the door, Chloe rubbed a hand gingerly over her belly, "Yeah ma." She looked up to eye her mother as she raised her chin in a show of superiority.

"We'll not be at war with the Blackbirds Chloe. I forbid it!"

Chloe stood frowning silently up at her mother. *You may not be at war mother, but I sure as hell am!*

Without a word, her mother turned and returned to her room leaving Chloe to try to figure out what had just happened. She crossed to the sofa, dropping onto the cushion as she wrapped her arms around herself. *What in the hell was that?* She rocked herself back and forth, as she replayed the incident in her mind.

Maybe he tripped. She shook her head. Dell had been standing motionless until his eyes had met hers.

She closed her eyes when she replayed the memory. Dell's dark eyes had erupted into a flame of blazing amber before his pupils had dilated to engulf his eyes moments before he'd dropped. She hadn't imagined it. Something had affected him.

Licking her lips, she stilled as she remembered the serenity that had washed over her. She'd felt so warm, so safe, so loved. It was like being whole. Like being home. God she wanted to feel it again, if only for a moment.

Chloe forced her eyes open as she gnashed her teeth. She refused to believe the emotion had anything to do with Dell Blackbird. *He can burn in hell!*

She forced herself to her feet. She knew her mother had gone back to bed, so she extinguished every light in the house before returning to the sofa to sit alone in the dark.

Chapter 3

Dell shifted once he hit the tree line. He had to get home, something was seriously wrong. The sudden attack that had disabled him at Chloe's door still had tremors coursing through his body. It had been her eyes. Something had happened when they locked eyes; he just had no idea what it was.

He half trotted, half limped through the dark forest, noting that the pain grew more intense the further from her he traveled.

Witch? He couldn't help but wonder if she and her family were some form of medicine people, magic makers. What else could explain what she'd done to him, because she had definitely *done* something.

Dell fell against the nearest tree and summoned his younger brother through pack ties that allowed them to communicate telepathically.

When Briggs confirmed that he was on his way, Dell pushed off the tree and forced himself onward. As much as it hurt and as much as he wanted to curl into a tight ball and wait for rescue, Dell was the Alpha now. With his brother's demise, he'd inherited the title as the eldest male sibling, and as Alpha he was expected to act as such. No cowering in the forest from a chance meeting with the sister of his brother's enemy.

Dell groaned as he forced himself forward. *If I could just stop thinking about her.* It seemed the pain lessened when he could force himself from thinking of her eyes. Those deep chocolate, almond shaped eyes that sparked with agony and anger. The memory had him doubling over. *Christ! Stop thinking about her!*

Curled into a ball of agony was how Briggs and Cindy found him minutes later.

"Dell, what's wrong?" Briggs shifted mid-stride and dropped to his brother's side.

Behind him Cindy shifted, but didn't approach.

"Not sure." Dell panted, trying to force more control than he actually possessed.

"You went to see *her* didn't you," Cindy accused from behind the brothers.

Briggs glanced over his shoulder, "Who?" He shifted his gaze from his sister back to his brother, "*Someone* did this to you?" Briggs rose to his full height, scanning the forest around them as he balled large hands into white knuckled fists. "Tell me who brother and I'll tear them apart!"

The rumble in his voice lasted only a fraction of a second before his words were cut off as Dell launched himself at his brother. "Don't ever fucking threaten *her!*"

Briggs didn't fight his brother, simply wrestled with him until another spasm of pain wracked Dell's body, forcing the Alpha to loosen his grip on his younger, yet larger brother.

Shocked, Briggs looked from Dell to Cindy. "What's wrong with him?"

Cindy stood motionless watching the display, her face ashen. *Oh God...the consequences!*

"Cindy!" Briggs prompted when she didn't answer.

I can't lose another brother. I won't! Cindy blinked and swallowed hard, "He's sick. It happens to all new Alphas."

Briggs didn't scent the lie, but Dell did. Since becoming Alpha, his senses were heightened, especially where it concerned his pack. He looked up from the forest floor, his eyes holding Cindy's for a moment.

He didn't have to say anything or communicate through the pack ties, she knew he'd want answers, and he'd want them soon. "Get him up Briggs; let's get him to the road."

Briggs tried to ease an arm around his brother, but Dell growled his dissent.

Alphas didn't need help. He'd requested their presence as standbys on the off chance that an enemy or predator were near. In his current state he was defenseless, and it was Cindy and Briggs' job as his siblings and his pack mates to watch his back when he was unwilling or unable to do the job himself.

Dell sucked in a sharp breath and forced himself forward. It might take a while, but he'd get back to the road and Briggs' truck by his own steam.

When Briggs pulled his truck up at the Blackbird compound he threw the shift in park and exited the vehicle crossing to assist Dell.

Again the Alpha growled at his Beta, shoving his brother's hands away.

"What's happened?"

Three heads looked up, startled to find their mother drying her hands on the hem of her apron at the back door.

"Nothing Mama," Cindy began, "Dell's just not feeling well."

Mama snorted once before frowning at her daughter. "Don't piss down my back and tell me it's raining young lady." Mama waited until Dell limped close enough for her to raise his chin with a finger forcing his eyes to meet hers. "You may be Alpha, but I'm the mother. Tell me what happened."

Dell jerked his chin from his mother's grasp, lifting his head as he strode past, "I don't know. I went to see Chloe and…"

Mama cut him off, "Chloe? The Lott girl?" Mama's eyes quickly scanned Dell's massive frame, "Did she hurt you son?"

Dell shook his head, "No she didn't. It was…something else."

Mama looked from Dell to Cindy knowingly, her old eyes lighting with a spark. She followed close on his heels. "What something? What was it?"

Cindy forced herself between Dell and Mama, "It was nothing. He's just sick, let it go."

Dell ignored his sister. "It was some sort of attack." He turned to eye his mother then, "It hit me so suddenly that I wasn't prepared. I was…incapacitated."

"When?" Mama demanded, "When did this *attack* hit?"

Dell shook his head, rubbing a large hand over the back of his neck. "I was at her door. She'd just answered. She must think I'm some kind of…" a low growl finished the sentence.

Mama was reaching for Dell when Cindy's words halted her. "It's just as well. They are our *enemies* Dell. There's no need for you to explain yourself to them." Cindy addressed Dell, but her eyes slid to her mothers, "Or any reason to ever see her again, it could only end badly."

Cindy didn't expect the angry growl that tore loose from her brother. "They are *not* our enemies!" Dell turned to frown at Briggs, "Call the pack."

"But brother..." Cindy began.

"CALL THE PACK!"

Briggs nodded once and disappeared to do his brother's bidding.

***

Lying on her mother's sofa, Chloe tried to will herself into sleep. Instead, an endless reel of the moment her eyes locked with Dell's played in a continuous loop over and over in her mind. She huffed out a harsh breath rolling to her side, annoyed with herself that she couldn't stop thinking of Dell. *They killed your brother idiot!*

It didn't matter and that angered her more than anything because it should have. But, the peace and serenity she found in his gaze had her yearning for a second encounter.

Sitting up, she shoved a hand through her hair. *It has to be fatigue.*

It was the only logical explanation. Her brother was dead by their hands and she couldn't stop thinking about how warm, relaxed, and safe she'd felt in Dell's presence.

Shoving up off the couch, she tiptoed upstairs to check on her still sleeping mother. She cracked the bedroom door a mere inch and peeked in, relieved to find her mother snoring heavily. Pushing the door open further she noted the open bottle of sleeping pills on her mother's night stand. She debated taking the bottle for only a moment before she decided she couldn't fault her mother for needing the sleeping aid. Hell, she should take a few and finally get some real sleep.

Instead, Chloe closed the door and went back downstairs to start a pot of coffee. If she couldn't sleep then she might as well try to be alert.

After filling the pot with water and a quadruple dose of coffee grounds, Chloe crossed her arms over her chest and rested one hip against the counter waiting for the maker to percolate.

Her lip curled in disgust as she remembered Cindy's words, *'You can come willingly, or I can make you.'* Chloe shook her head in disgust, "I shoulda dropped that bitch on her ass."

She'd known the Blackbirds forever. Well known *of* them. They were a large family. There were only four siblings, Mace, Dell, Cindy, and Briggs, but they had countless aunts, uncles, nieces, and nephews that also spent a great deal of time at the Blackbird compound. Not to mention that they themselves had recently started procreating. Cindy and her husband Michael had a two year old son, and it was rumored that Briggs, in a serious relationship of his own, was on the verge of proposing to his girlfriend Jessika.

She'd decided years ago that the closeness of the family was one of the greatest contributing factors to the whole shape-shifter myth surrounding the Blackbirds. No one ever, *ever* encountered a Blackbird out alone. The family always traveled in packs. It was odd.

Chloe's lips curled into a smile, *Maybe they have social anxiety. That'd explain Dell's behavior today.*

She poured herself a steaming mug of coffee and dropped into a chair at the kitchen bar, not bothering with cream or sugar. *Dell.* God, how she'd fantasized about him. When her family had first moved to the area she'd had the biggest crush on him. It was her senior year of high school, but the year had come and gone so quickly she never had the chance to approach him. Not that she would have. It would have been humiliating. Dell, like Mace before him and Briggs behind him, was the most handsome boy in his class. Any Blackbird son had his pick of the school girls, and Chloe hadn't been confident enough in neither her looks nor personality to even think of approaching Dell.

Her lips quirked again, it didn't mean she hadn't caught him checking her out a time or two, but an exchange of glances across the cafeteria was as far as it had ever gone.

She remembered coming home from school one spring day to find Donnie pacing on the front porch, "Hey," he'd yelled as she approached. "If I catch Dell Blackbird staring at your ass again, I'm gonna put him in the ground."

When Donnie would have had the opportunity to catch Dell checking her out she had no idea, but the fact that her brother had, meant that she hadn't been imagining the glances from Dell. She hadn't slept for days after the revelation, but Dell graduated early and she hadn't seen him again for years. She'd gone off to college and lord only knew where he'd gone. She hadn't seen him again until he'd strode into Donnie's funeral. She hated to admit it, but he had actually grown more handsome. His once unruly impossibly dark hair that always seemed to be in his eyes, was now shorn and brushed back without a hair out of place. *But still black as pitch*, Chloe mused. She'd always remembered him as a lithe muscular jock, but it seemed his frame had doubled in size. He was taller, with much broader shoulders, but cut and well defined. *Too well defined.* His mere presence in the room demanded attention and female appreciation.

God what would Donnie think? As if summoned up by the flash of pain that stole through her and compressed her heart in a painful spasm, the dark room suddenly lit with blinding light as thunder cracked the sky and sent lightening streaking across the heavens.

Chloe clenched a hand to her chest hoping the pain would pass even as a sob tore loose, and like the rain now flowing in steady rivulets down the glass windows, her tears sprang free.

God I hate him! I FUCKING HATE THEM! It was all their fault. They had to have everything. The Blackbirds weren't used to being told 'No', so when her brother had stood firm and protected his wife they had destroyed him for it. Chloe squeezed her eyes tight against the pain.

Donnie and Beverly had been married a mere two years when Beverly had gotten lost in the mountains on a weekend camping trip with the girls. Donnie had been devastated when he'd heard. He formed his own search party and scoured the mountain against the wishes of the local law enforcement. Chloe had joined his crew and they'd retraced the parties' path all the way back to the campground. They'd searched for two days straight before the snow came and forced them back down the mountain. Donnie had only called it quits because she'd threatened to stay too.

The next morning the police came for Donnie at his mother's home, they'd found Beverly. Rather, Mace Blackbird had found her. She was dehydrated and near hypothermic, but alive. And that's when everything changed.

Mace checked on Beverly in the hospital and continued to do so, even visiting her at her and Donnie's home once she was well. Out of gratitude Donnie didn't mind at first, but Beverly was disappearing to see Mace. The relationship had all the signs of an affair except for the fact the Beverly swore she and Mace were just friends.

Chloe knew differently. She watched them together, saw the way Mace looked at Beverly the way he protected her, the way his jaw clenched when Donnie would touch her. Chloe had confronted her, telling her that if she didn't want her brother to let him go rather than string him along.

'But I love him', Beverly had cried. 'With all my soul Chloe, I love your brother. I'm just confused. I need time. I want this to work.'

Chloe could tell then that Beverly was losing sleep over the whole ordeal.

Donnie asked Mace to stay away and he did so begrudgingly. At first Beverly was thankful, then resentful. Then it was discovered that Mace hadn't stayed away at all. He and Beverly were meeting in secret.

Chloe had begged Donnie to let her go, get a divorce, but Donnie refused. As a result of all the drama, his work began to suffer and the foreman had threatened to let him go. Finally it all came to a head and Donnie drove out to the Blackbird compound and confronted Mace only to discover Beverly there. Donnie and Mace fought and Donnie had been injured. Donnie spent the night in the hospital, Mace spent the night in jail and Beverly spent the night downing sleeping pills and a bottle of vodka.

When Chloe drove Donnie home from the hospital late the next night they found Beverly's body. She was lying in their bed holding her wedding ring in her hand. She'd been dead for hours, but it didn't keep Donnie from trying to resuscitate her.

Chloe remembered thinking then and there that nothing in the world could ever be more painful than watching your loved ones suffer. She'd been wrong. Losing a loved one after they'd been made to suffer was more heart wrenching than she could have ever possibly imagined.

Beverly's body wasn't even carried from the house before Donnie was gone, hunting down Mace. No one knew exactly what happened, but the bodies of both men were found the next day. The county Sheriff believed Donnie had shot Mace and then had been attacked by wolves. It all sounded too crazy. There were whispers that the shape shifting Blackbird pack had discovered Mace dead and had torn Donnie apart. The coroner must have heard the rumors as well, for he assured Chloe and her mother that Donnie had died from wounds sustained from a lone wolf, not a pack. 'A lucky shot' he'd called it, 'the one bite ripped through Donnie's jugular'.

"Lucky for who?" Chloe had snarled in anguish.

Thunder again rattled the sky. The great boom shaking the windows on the house, and Chloe cried all the harder because she knew no one would hear, no one would comfort, and no one would ever know that her heart had been ripped free of her soul.

She now knew how Donnie had felt staring at the lifeless body of his beloved wife. She too wanted revenge. She wanted one of them to hurt like she hurt, hate as she now hated, suffer as she suffered. She'd lost her sister-in-law and her brother. They'd only lost one.

It's not fair! She pounded a fist on the table as thunder cracked again. It felt so good to hit something. She pounded her fist on the table harder and then kept on pounding until she couldn't pound anymore.

Chapter 4

At the Blackbird compound, Dell was having an equally restless night as the new Alpha. He'd given his pack the last five days to come to terms with the loss of their Alpha. He knew their sorrow and anger needed time, but he knew now that he needed to act to prevent any of them from seeking revenge. He'd summoned his pack and given direct orders that no member of the Lott family was to be harmed or treated with animosity. The pack was to stay away from the Lotts at all cost. The pack hadn't taken it well. They missed Mace and they wanted closure for their former Alpha's sake. Little did they know that not only was Dell keeping the Lott family safe, but his pack as well. Until he figured out the cause of his attack on Chloe's doorstep, he didn't want his pack getting too close to the woman or her mother.

Dell heaved a great sigh and rolled to his side to stare out the window and into the dreary night. It was late, but sleep refused to claim him. Hell, he missed Mace more than any of them ever would.

He'd been the quintessential little brother. One corner of his mouth lifted. He'd hounded Mace for years until Briggs came into his own and followed suit with Dell. After seeing how annoying pesky little brothers could be, Dell had reined it in, but he hadn't been so lucky with Briggs. Briggs was the baby after all and was therefore never afforded the opportunity to be harassed incessantly by a younger sibling, so he saw no problem with annoying Dell at every possible opportunity.

He'd sensed at the meeting that Briggs had taken umbrage with Dell's directive, but his little brother would do as he was told for it was his job to lead by example when it came to showing respect and submission to the new Alpha's orders.

Cindy, on the other hand, had snuck out before the meeting was over; leaving Dell unable to question her about the information she was obviously keeping from him. When the meeting concluded and he'd explained himself more thoroughly to a few of the more *emotional* pack members, he'd opted to let Cindy have this one. He'd get the information she was harboring from her in the morning. He was Alpha now, and as a member of his pack, Cindy was obligated to conform to his wishes, which included supplying him with any and all information he sought. He could have just contacted her telepathically, or—as he'd recently discovered—gotten access to her thoughts without her permission, but he wanted to be a fair leader, a just Alpha, and that meant giving her the opportunity to do the right thing.

He rubbed a hand over his firm abdomen, grateful that the queasiness had finally subsided. It was an effort even now, to keep from thinking about Chloe Lott and whatever it was that she had done to him. He prayed for her sake that it wasn't some form of medicine, or that it wasn't intentionally done. He could literally scent her pain from a mile away and he knew from personal experience that pain that great often led to extremely foolish decisions.

Chloe. His gut spasmed at the mere thought of her. Growling against the pain, he allowed himself to remember. He had forgotten about her. Forgotten he'd been *interested* in her.

She'd caught his eye in high school, and it wasn't her beauty that attracted him. And God had she been beautiful. His abdomen squeezed tighter. *She still is.* No, he'd been drawn to her character. She was new to the school. Where most teenage girls to a new area would have been doing their damnedest to get in with the 'it crowd', Chloe hadn't. She seemed disinterested in the social sects of the high school and even less concerned with anyone else's opinion of her. His lips curled despite the pain in his belly. He remembered the day she'd arrived.

He was late for algebra and was racing for his homeroom when he saw her scanning a class assignment card at the end of the hall. She was eyeing the numbers at the top of each door, clearly lost. He intended on stopping to point her in the right direction when her shout had his feet skidding to a halt.

"Hey! Leave him alone!"

She was frowning down a hallway and when she disappeared down it, Dell raced to see what was happening. He was more than a little shocked to find her standing in the hall, hands on slender hips, scowling up at a senior football player that towered at least three feet taller. At her feet, a wiry underclassman with broken glasses was picking up a pile of books.

"You're so tough? Why don't you try picking on someone your own size?"

The football player snorted and took a challenging step closer to her. "Would that be you?"

Watching, Dell expected Chloe to back down but she didn't. Instead, she stepped closer to the boy. Whatever her retort would have been Dell never found out.

"No, that'd be me," He'd answered as he strode toward the trio.

Dell didn't know the football player, but he apparently knew Dell because he instantly threw up his hands and backed down the hall, "Look I don't want any trouble. It was an accident." The boy kept walking backward until he reached the end of the hall then he turned and disappeared down the corridor.

He didn't like bullies; despised them actually. While part of him wanted to chase the kid down and pound him into the ground, he opted instead to stay and offer the nerdy underclassman a hand.

He turned to find Chloe already on her knees helping to collect the books that were strewn about the hall.

"You alright?" she asked the kid.

"F-fine. Thanks for your help. No one's ever stuck up for me like that before."

He watched as Chloe rose and placed the few books she had on the kid's towering pile. Dell remembered wondering how the kid's pale boney arms were even able to endure the weight.

"My name is Chloe Lott."

The nerdy kid simply nodded, "I'm Jerry. Thanks for your help."

"Anytime," Chloe smiled, "and thank you." She'd turned to smile at Dell.

"Sure," he supplied lamely before a teacher had shouted from down the hall for the trio to "Get to class!"

He didn't want to go, but then Chloe stepped to a door, double-checked her class assignment card and entered it leaving him alone in the hall with the nerd.

"You need help with that," he'd asked the underclassman.

When the kid confirmed that he could handle his load, Dell double-timed it to class and spent the remainder of the day thinking about the new girl who wasn't afraid to challenge the bully.

After that day he'd watched her incessantly, wondering if her temporary lapse in sanity was a fluke. It wasn't. She defended the 'little guy' at every opportunity that presented itself and it was more than a little intriguing.

He watched her constantly, even shifting to follow her home under the cover of the woods. Hell, her brother had even caught him ogling her ass a time or two. When he'd finally built up the nerve to finally ask her out, it had been too late.

The change that affects all shifters had come upon him suddenly and it hit him hard. So hard in fact that Mama was forced to pull him from school. He'd been forced to finish his senior year in the confines of the Blackbird compound. Convinced he'd fallen ill with some mysterious ailment, the school officials were more than willing to cooperate. Cindy spread the word that he'd graduated early and that was that. High school was over.

The change in him had taken so much time, energy, and patience that he'd soon given up on ever seeing Chloe again. By the time he'd mastered his abilities, it was too late. She'd already graduated and moved on. Even if she hadn't, he wouldn't have pursued her. He'd had a difficult enough time coming to terms with what he was; he'd have been unable to explain it to anyone else.

Chloe wasn't the only thing he'd missed out on. He'd been a national wrestling champion, but was forced to quit the team and refuse all thirteen of the scholarships that he'd been offered.

"You're different son," Mama had told him, "our destiny is not that of the average man. You have responsibilities."

He'd always known that they were different, that they were shifters, but it wasn't until he came into his own abilities that he'd realized just how different they were. While his brothers and sister dated, he'd shied away from it. He didn't want to drag anyone into his life, especially someone he cared for. Those first years of coming to terms with what he was had him questioning his own existence, and while things got better with time his life was still certainly something he wouldn't wish on any child or non-shifter mate of his own.

Mate of his own. Chloe. God, why couldn't Mace have mated another woman, any other woman. No, he'd gone after the only possible option that was destined to draw Chloe back into his life in the most deplorable manner possible. *It's hopeless.*

Chapter 5

Chloe woke feeling just as crappy as she had when she'd finally fallen asleep a mere three hours earlier.

She made her mother a quick breakfast of jelly toast, scrambled eggs, and coffee before deserting her at the kitchen table to sneak off to what was once her bedroom but was now used by her mother as a makeshift sewing room.

Chloe rummaged through a sack of her old clothes she found in the closet. Her mother kept them on hand because as she liked to say, "You never know when one of my babies is gonna have to come home unprepared."

Finding a faded pair of yoga pants, an old gray hockey t-shirt, and a dingy pair of tennis shoes, Chloe dressed quickly. After beating the hell out of her mother's dining table the night before, she'd discovered that her anger and pain desperately needed an outlet, and apparently none was more therapeutic than physical exertion.

The sky was still overcast when she finally pecked her mother on the cheek and double-timed it down the front steps to the road. A light fog hung in air and swirled her breath as she exhaled. The infinitesimal droplets felt refreshing on her face. She took a deep breath in, thankful as of late for every breath of fresh Montana air she could get. In the past few days it seemed a great weight had settled itself in the center of her chest, keeping her from breathing deeply or even comfortably for that matter. But occasionally, she stopped and forced herself to breathe deep, to take in the glory of fresh, clean, mountain air.

Popping in her ear buds, she scanned her I-pod as she walked briskly toward the outskirts of town. There was an excellent path through the woods not too far from the house. It wasn't intended as a jogging path, but she craved the challenge and the solitude.

She hit play on her I-pod and was delighted to find it already set to the perfect running song. *30 Seconds to Mars, how fitting. This whole life is nothing but one big beautiful fucking lie.*

She didn't wait to hit the path to break into a run; instead she turned the I-pod as loud as it would go and loped to the woods.

Once she hit the tree line and was certain she wasn't being watched, she broke into a dead run. She raced up and around the curved path that led up the steep mountain side. Her steps didn't falter. She hurdled downed tree branches and side-stepped large mud holes. Her arms and legs pumped furiously and her heart beat just as hard to keep up. When the song ended she hit repeat and forced herself on harder. After a few minutes she didn't have to concentrate on the path anymore, instead her thoughts went to her brother. When the block of ice threatened to encase her heart she pushed herself harder and faster praying to outrun the pain even as she forced her thoughts from the painful loss of her brother to the easier to manipulate hatred she harbored for Dell Blackbird.

The fucking nerve of him to think he had any right showing his face at my brother's funeral! Her cheeks burned with anger and exertion. She gritted her teeth and pushed harder, faster. Somewhere she'd stopped trying to dodge the mud puddles and now blazed through them, sending brown murky water shooting up to cover her pants and light blue jacket.

'It's a beautiful lie. It's a perfect denial. Such a beautiful lie to believe in...'

Tears threatened and still she pushed herself impossibly harder, not even slowing to unzip her jacket and toss it aside not even caring whether she found it on her trek back home.

'It's time to forget about the past, to wash away what happened last. Hide behind an empty face, don't ask too much just say...cause this is just a game'

She ran hard even as she fought to retain control over her emotions. She'd had so little control over anything in the past few days; surely, she could control herself, her heart. It was all she had left.

Such a beautiful lie to believe in. It's a beautiful, beautiful LIE MAKES ME...

She fell to her knees, sliding through the mud for several feet before her fists curled deep into the earth forcing soil hard under her nails. The pain of it felt good, a refreshing reprieve from the pain in her heart that she could do nothing to cure. She fought to hold back her emotion to suck it down, but it wasn't the pain that sent her over the edge it was the anger.

On her hands and knees, hip deep in wet earth she threw back her head and screamed with all the misery and rage a soul could expel. "AAAAAAAAAAAAAAH!"

Why? Why couldn't she have saved her brother? Why hadn't she seen it coming?

"Aaaaah!" Sobs wracked her body as she pulled her fists back and crossed them over her chest. *Please God let the ache stop!* She sucked in a breath as warm tears stole down her cheeks, "Please just fucking stop!"

She lifted a muddy hand to cover her mouth, while the other ripped out her ear buds. She sat rocking back and forth and simply cried. She cried until feeling all the pain, anger, and hatred left her exhausted. Taking in a long breath, she laughed through her tears at herself. How in the hell would she explain her appearance to her mother?

She jumped when heard a rustling behind her. Spinning quickly, embarrassment stole through her at the spectacle she knew she would be to any passerby.

At first she was relieved to see a large dog standing in the tree line, but her relief quickly faded when she realized it wasn't a dog at all. It was a huge gray wolf.

Fuck! She scanned her surroundings quickly searching for a stick, or branch, or rock, or anything resembling a weapon. She found none. She slowly rose to her feet remembering an article she'd read somewhere that animals didn't like to attack anything larger than them. *Shit, that was bears...wasn't it?*

She took a tentative step backwards, her eyes still scanning the area for a weapon even as she noted the posture of the wolf. *Tail's not wagging, definitely not a good sign. Or is that only for dogs? God why didn't I pay attention to that damn wolf biography on the nature channel?*

It felt a little odd to have her heart clenching from an emotion other than anger and sadness. Chloe took another step backward even as she thought. *Is it sad that fear is a little invigorating?*

Her heel caught on a root and unable to catch herself, she dropped to her ass with a wet thud. When the wolf took a step closer she scrambled backward until her back hit a tree and that's when it happened.

Her eyes locked with the wolf's and that same peaceful serenity she'd felt the night before staring at Dell engulfed her. The wolf stepped closer and Chloe slumped back against the tree resignedly, no longer caring whether the beast intended to tear her to shreds. She couldn't tear her eyes from his.

Again that same warm amber gaze stole her torture, leaving her at peace. *Maybe he's going to kill me,* she thought with little emotion. *Maybe this is the peacefulness that people say washes over you just before you die.*

If it was, she didn't care. She'd welcome death if it meant feeling this tranquility forever.

When the wolf approached, Chloe lifted a tentative hand and held her breath. The wolf seemed to notice, but didn't take his eyes from her. When she buried her fingers deep in the thick matte of grey fur they both jumped. Chloe grasped her wrist against the electric shock she'd felt. She stared at the wolf that retreated to the tree-line before she scrambled to her feet. She didn't look back as she made a mad dash down the hill side. She cut through the woods until she found the path, her head felt fuzzy, but she shook it off and raced as fast as her legs could carry her. She didn't hear the wolf in pursuit, but that didn't mean she had any intentions of slowing.

At the bottom of the hill she dashed out into the road and had to jump back just as quickly as a car sped past sounding its horn loudly, perturbed at her idiocy.

She turned and huffed great sawing breaths as she eyed the forest. No sign of the wolf, but just to be safe she walked the shoulder of the road all the way back to town.

By the time she arrived at her mother's she was shivering. Her arms clamped tightly around her, she'd had designs on hosing herself off before going in, but opted against it. The last thing her mother needed was to have to take care of a sick daughter.

Chloe eased the front door open, toeing off her muddy running shoes just outside the front door. She was tiptoeing through the sitting room when her mother's voice halted her.

"Jesus! What happened to you?"

Chloe stilled, righting her hunched shoulders as she turned to eye her mother then dropped her eyes to her mud encrusted running clothes. "Oh…uh nothing. Well, something." She lifted her eyes and caught a hint of her mother's growing impatience as she stumbled on, "I went for a jog on the mountain path and I tripped on a branch."

Bea crossed her arms over her chest. "Tripped on a branch or got beat up by it?"

Chloe rolled her eyes turning her back to stalk towards the stairs, "Oh mom! I just fell. It's slippery."

Chloe was halfway up the stairs when her mother yelled, "Where's your jacket? You didn't wear a jacket? Why wouldn't you wear a jacket?"

Chloe lifted a hand and shook her head opening her mouth for a defense, but none came. "I'm gonna hit the shower," she offered lamely then she turned and was gone.

***

Dell hadn't moved. From the moment Chloe ran from the forest, he'd stood transfixed. *What have we done?*

He thought the death of his eldest brother was the worst pain he'd ever be called upon to endure, but he'd been wrong. Watching Chloe have her break down alone in the forest had been more than painful to watch, it had been excruciating. Never in his life had he wanted to heal another's suffering as much as he wanted to heal hers. She'd been so strong, fought so hard to maintain her self-control. Much like him, she'd only afforded herself the luxury of exhibiting any real emotion when she thought she'd been utterly alone. She was so much like him. He too had stayed strong as new Alpha. His newly claimed pack relied on him, watched him for signs of weakness, and he'd given them none. But it didn't mean that he hadn't shifted at night and run miles into the woods to howl his misery at the ever constant moon.

Yes he'd suffered, but not like her. Her cry had been so painful to watch that his throat had thickened with emotion, making it nearly impossible for him to swallow down his anger. He'd never been so angry. He'd wanted to hunt down whoever had caused Chloe's misery and rip their fucking throat out but how could he when *his* family had been the cause.

Self-condemnation rolled through him in persistent waves leaving him nauseous with the guilt. *I should have shifted, should have held her.*

Even as he thought it, he knew it would have been impossible. Whatever spell or medicine she'd used on him still hadn't dissipated. When she'd touched him, it had been just as agonizing as when he'd first met her eyes.

Unable to stand any longer, he sat. His amber wolfs eyes staring unseeingly into the forest. He couldn't get over how beautiful she'd been. Dropped in the mud covered in earth, sweat, and tears, and he hadn't been able to tear his eyes from her.

Has she always been so beautiful? Why hadn't he remembered? Surely, he should have remembered just how unbelievably breathtaking she was. Maybe it was the witchcraft she'd been using on him. *Mates?* He quickly discarded the thought as quickly as it was taken up. *Love spell? But why? She'd have no desire to bind herself to her enemies in any intimate manner.*

Dell sobered then, rising quickly. *Unless she wants me to suffer as she feels her brother had suffered. To be bound to a mate that would never be mine, a mate that would never allow a claiming.* Dell's jaw began to work as he gnashed his teeth. *Deceitful little...* He turned then and raced back to the Blackbird compound.

Chapter 6

Shuffling down the isle of the local supermarket, Chloe picked up a can of artichoke hearts and eyed it unseeingly before she slid it back on the shelf. Her mother had demanded to go to the market even though Chloe protested. "It's too soon," she'd argued to her mother who in turn snatched up her coat and said, "Too soon for groceries? That doesn't make sense."

Tired of waiting for her mother who'd disappeared to retrieve a pound of jalapenos, Chloe abandoned her position in the canned veggies aisle and set off in pursuit of her mother.

She searched aisle after aisle until her mother's familiar voice could be heard from nearby. Chloe followed the sound, turning into the produce aisle and locking eyes with Dell Blackbird. He was standing in front of her mother, smiling pleasantly. Chloe noted how his smile faltered when he saw her. How had he known she was coming? He wasn't surprised to see her. His eyes were already locked on the spot she'd stepped into before she'd stepped into it. It was as if he was, *Waiting for me?*

Frowning at him, she couldn't explain the warmth that seeped into her bones. She felt like she'd just eased herself into a steaming hot bath. She blinked then realized she'd let her eyes linger closed for just a fraction too long. When she opened her eyes again Dell was staring at her strangely. For a moment she considered retreating, but when her mother's eyes followed Dell's gaze she lifted a hand to Chloe.

"Chloe, come say hello to Dell."

Fuck! Chloe didn't bother plastering on a fake smile. Dell knew how she felt about him, pretense wasn't necessary. Approaching her mother's side, Chloe said nothing.

Dell extended his hand, "We haven't been formerly introduced. I'm Dell Blackbird."

Chloe simply stared at him for several tense moments before her mother's elbow in her ribs had her reaching out to shake Dell's hand.

When his fingers closed solidly around hers, Chloe thought she caught a wince flash across his stern features, but the thought was only momentary when her own buckling knees had her reaching out for something solid to steady herself.

"Chloe!" her mother gasped.

Dell reached out, enfolding her in his strong arms as he pulled her close.

Shocked, Chloe held his gaze as she struggled to regain her legs. For some inexplicable reason, her muscles felt like melted butter. Struggling to right herself, her legs and arms began to tremble with the effort. "I'm fine," she ground out trying to pull from Dell's embrace. "Let me go."

"Should I call someone?" Her mother was near hysterical.

"No ma!" Chloe pushed against the wall of Dell's chest and tore her eyes from his even as she saw the muscle in his jaw twitch. "I'm fine. I'm…" she couldn't explain it so she grabbed the first logical excuse that sprang to mind, "just exhausted. I think I ran too far this morning." She could feel Dell's eyes on her. Without looking up she pushed at the solid wall of his chest again. "You can let me go."

Dell extended his arms, holding her from him but keeping his hands firmly locked on her upper arms. "Are you okay?"

Annoyed now she jerked out of his grasp, "Fine! Thanks!" Her eyes flicked up to her mothers, "I'm going to the car. Take your time."

Even as she stalked toward the exit she could hear her mother's concern, "Chloe wait!"

"It's fine Ms. Lott, I'll make sure she gets safely to the car."

Chloe quickened her step at Dell's words.

"Oh thank you Dell. I'll just check out and be right there."

Chloe squeezed through the automatic doors before they had even fully opened. When the brisk Montana air hit her, she inhaled deeply unaware that the air in the store had become so stifling. She didn't look behind her as she eyed the parking lot searching for her car. She stepped off the curb and heard a horn sound loudly before she was jerked back.

"What in the hell is wrong with you!" Dell growled at her ear.

With his arms wrapped around her, her knees once again gave out. *What in the fuck is happening?* Perspiration dotted her nose as her body suddenly ignited in a flood of warmth. Something was definitely wrong. *The flu?*

When Dell spun her and swept her up into his arms, she wanted to struggle but when her eyes locked with his her vision blurred and sent the world spinning violently around her.

She heard Dell curse and she tried to focus on his face. He too was flushed and sweating. Was she that heavy? When his eyes locked on hers, there was a bright flash. Flooded by light, she squinted, but it only grew brighter and brighter. The light was blinding, and when she closed her eyes against it, they didn't reopen.

***

"You didn't see it Cindy. She fainted right there in my arms and it was literally physically painful for me. You're certain it's not medicine?" Dell demanded.

Cindy shrugged negligently, "There's no way to be sure. Best bet is just to stay the hell away from her."

Dell groaned in annoyance, "I want to, but for some fucking reason I'm drawn to her. She's all I think about." He shook his head. "It's gotta be medicine, but if it is I don't understand why it would have such a negative effect on her." He stood then, storming from his office. "Where's mama?"

Cindy chased after him, "She's gone to Great Falls to spend a few days with Aunty Connie."

"Christ!" the word came out as a growl. "Extremely poor timing. Get on the phone and get her back."

"She needs this break Briggs." Cindy's eyes turned imploring, "She's still not over the loss of Mace and she just needs a vacation. Let her have some time with her sister." She knew it was cheap, but she'd do whatever was called for to keep Dell safe.

Dell rolled his shoulders in an effort to relieve some of the tension that had been building there for the past few days. He took a deep breath and let it out slowly. "Let her stay. It'll just," his brows furrowed, "have to wait."

Cindy smiled then, "Don't worry brother, by the time she gets home I'm sure your...*illness* will have passed."

Dell merely grunted before returning to his desk. "What do you know of medicine? How do I break it?"

Yes! "Distance," she answered too eagerly. "You need to stay as far from her for as long as possible. Her medicine won't work if you don't come in contact with her."

"And you know this how?" Dell asked hoisting his hiking-boot clad feet up onto the desk.

"*I* actually pay attention to the stories Mama tells."

"*Stories,*" Dell emphasized, "it doesn't mean any of it is true."

Cindy let her eyes slide over her brother condescendingly, "True enough to be affecting you."

***

It had been a few hours and Chloe's cheeks still stung with the humiliation of being carried across the parking lot of the local supermarket by Dell.

"Are you sure you're alright hon? We could go to the E.R."

"I'm fine ma!" Chloe snapped a little too rudely before amending, "Look I'm sorry I'm just...it was pretty embarrassing."

"What is there to be embarrassed about? You fainted. So what! You should be thankful that fine young man was there to catch you."

With the memory Chloe's cheeks once again flamed. "God mom, can we please just stop talking about it? I told you it was just exertion, I'm not sick." Then as an afterthought, "And Dell isn't a fine young man."

Her mother pursed her lips, "I am entitled to my opinion."

"Look, I'm going to lie down for a while."

"That's a good idea."

Now it was Chloe's turn to purse her lips, "Are you going to be okay?"

"I'll be fine. I'll start some dinner and wake you when it's ready."

Chloe eased herself up off the couch her mother had been forcing her to lie on for the past two hours. She wasn't tired in the least, but going upstairs and pretending to nap had to be better than being scrutinized by her mother every ten seconds.

"Hold on to the railing," her mother's chastised.

Rolling her eyes, Chloe was tempted to take the stairs two-at-a-time, but inevitably decided against it. As annoying as her mother could be, she knew she only meant well.

In the guest bedroom, Chloe quietly closed the door and crossed to the bed before snagging the remote and plopping down to channel surf.

The room was quite plain. White plush carpet covered the floor and the large bed, adorned with a satiny plum comforter, rested against the wall under the window. Only one painting hung on the wall. It was an oil painting her mother had done in an art class she'd taken years ago. The scene depicted two quaking aspens reaching up to a blue cloud dotted sky with majestic purple peaks in the background.

Chloe eyed the painting. It was quite good really. When a commercial came blaring onto the screen she cringed and quickly pressed the button to reduce the volume. She didn't want her mother racing up to ensure she was actually napping. Holding her breath and listening for several tense moments, she only exhaled once she was certain her mother wasn't pounding up the stairs to check on her.

Christ! She closed her eyes and listened to the low murmur of voices coming from the screen. They were talking about food. *The cooking network?* Ever since her spell earlier in the day she'd been unable to concentrate on anything except the mortification of the event. But now, finally alone and able to actually sit and think about it she couldn't help but wonder if something were in fact wrong with her.

She'd been fine earlier in the day. She'd eaten, slept as well as could be expected, but when she'd gotten near Dell. It was him! Something about him triggered her episode and it only worsened when he touched her. *Maybe it's my animosity.* She'd never hated a family more in her life. *That must be it.* Her hatred coupled with the recent loss of her brother and being back home. It had to be a culmination of everything. She sighed heavily, not entirely convinced she'd accurately diagnosed the source of her fainting spell. Regardless, there was little else that made sense. It couldn't have been triggered by Dell or his touch. That was ridiculous. *Right?* She was still trying to figure it out when her mother finally called her down to dinner nearly an hour later.

Chapter 7

The next day was spent consistently confirming to her mother that she wasn't ill or injured.

"For the hundredth time ma, I'm fine."

"Healthy people don't just faint for no apparent reason Chloe. It's not normal. You're sure you won't go see a doctor, if even just to appease your mother?"

"It's been a long stressful week mom. I forgot to eat after my run and I haven't been sleeping. Please just give me a few days to get back into a routine and if anything like that happens again, I swear I'll go get checked out."

Bea eyed her daughter doubtfully and huffed in obvious displeasure, "Well, if that's as good as I'm gonna get I'll have to take it."

By that evening, Chloe couldn't stand to be holed up any longer. She threw on her tennis shoes and snagged the grocery list from where it hung by a magnet on the fridge. "Ma, I'm heading to the grocery store."

Bea was settled in front of the TV. Some sitcom was blaring, but Bea wasn't watching it as she knitted a long woolen scarf. "But we went yesterday," she protested.

"Yeah, but you only got enough stuff for dinner when we had to rush out. I'll just go grab the rest of the items on your list."

Bea set down her knitting and hooked her pointer finger through the wire bridge of her glasses to tug them lower as she dropped her head and peered over the lenses at her daughter. "Maybe I should come with you."

"No ma, I'll be right in and right out." Chloe snatched her jacket off the hook and hung it over one arm.

"What if something happens?"

Chloe rolled her eyes, "Like what? I drop a jar of pickles? Clean up on aisle seven."

The joke was lost on her mother, "What if you have another spell and neither Dell nor I are there to save you?"

Chloe gritted her teeth at the mere mention of his name. She hated how her mother used it so casually in a sentence, like he was part of the family or something. "He didn't save me mom."

She jerked open the front door, talking rapidly as she went to keep her mother from cutting in, "Look, I'll be back in twenty-minutes. If I'm going to take longer I'll call. Plus I've eaten today and slept well last night so I should be fine." The lies rolled off her tongue smoothly as she stepped out the door and closed it behind her.

Christ! What's a girl gotta do to get some shopping done? Honestly, the shopping wasn't her true agenda. She simply couldn't bear to be in the house any longer. She felt useless just sitting around sulking in her misery. It was even more offensive because she couldn't stop thinking about her encounter with Dell.

At the grocery store, she winced as she strode past the area where she'd fainted the day before. Images of herself being carried across the parking lot in Dell's arms instantly flooded her even as she tried to force them back.

Inside she grabbed a cart and pulled the grocery list out of her purse. She'd made the list herself upon her arrival at her mothers. Her mom had a terrible habit of buying groceries as she needed them rather than stocking up all at once.

Halfway through her shopping, she stopped in the frozen food section. She grabbed a box of frozen waffles and a bag of pre-formed dinner rolls when something had her bristling. Despite the cool temperature of the freezer she stood in, her elbow propping open the door, she was suddenly flooded by a familiar warmth. It was the same warmth that had consumed her the day before. Panic struck, *Oh God, don't do this again. Not now!* She turned to eye the aisle. *Not here!* When she turned she tensed. Her escalated breathing fogged the chilled glass of the freezer door. *Did I just see what I think I saw?"* She lifted a hand and swiped it slowly down the glass clearing the foggy glass to reveal Dell standing at the end of the aisle staring directly at her.

Fuck! She stepped back, letting the door slam closed as she gripped her cart and steered it in the opposite direction. She kept her eyes down, hoping he hadn't noticed that she'd seen him.

When she cleared the aisle, her arms were literally shaking. She took deep breaths trying to calm herself as she skipped four aisles, opting to put some distance between herself and Dell.

Clearly they'd both not gotten any shopping done yesterday and had decided to finish it up today. *Great!* She considered leaving and coming back tomorrow, but knew it would heighten her mother's suspicion so much that she'd be forced to confess to a second encounter with Dell. *I am not doing that!*

Deciding to stand her ground and just ignore him if she saw him again, Chloe cruised down the aisle at a supermarket sweeper's pace. She snatched a jar of peanut butter as she quickly passed by. She didn't stop to peruse brands or debate on chunky or smooth, she simply grabbed the first jar she saw and kept on walking.

She finished three aisles in this manner. In the fourth, she grabbed a jar of cherries and froze as the warm sensation swept over her again. She looked up and was relieved to find the aisle in front of her empty.

"How are you?"

Dell's voice behind her had her tensing.

She didn't answer at first, but turned to find him towering directly behind her. "What do you want?" She watched as his dreamy amber eyes slid up and down her frame, making her suddenly self-conscious about her attire. She hadn't intended on leaving the house that day so she'd dressed comfortably that morning in a pair of old, form fitting jeans that were ripped high on each thigh. Her white t-shirt was just as old, and the way it stretched too tight across her breasts was a testament to her smaller size of yesteryear. The only thing that was even close to suitable for a day out were the new white tennis shoes that shone too brightly on her small feet. She fidgeted uncomfortably and turned away from Dell when his gaze lingered a fraction too long on her breasts. "Good bye Dell."

"Wait."

Chloe looked back just in time to see him reach for her. She jumped back and in doing so dropped the jar of cherries she held, sending a loud crash reverberating through the aisle. Her eyes were large as she scowled up at him, "Don't touch me!"

A store employee arrived in the aisle just as Chloe said the words. The employee was large, and thick, reminding her of one of the wise-guys she'd seen on a TV show about the mob. He wasn't close to being as large and muscular as Dell, but he didn't seem deterred.

The employee stopped and eyed Chloe then focused on Dell. "You alright lady? This guy bothering you?"

"I'm fine," Chloe kept her scowl on Dell, "he was just leaving."

Dell tore his eyes from Chloe and didn't even look at the employee as he turned in the opposite direction and stormed angrily down the aisle.

Chloe watched Dell stalk away. Even with his jacket on, she could see the muscles of his back and arms bunch. Her belly fluttered. *Why does he have this effect on me?* She'd forgotten all about the store employee until he crossed in front of her and dropped to a knee to start picking up the larger chunks of broken glass.

"I'm sorry, it just slipped."

"That's alright," the employee kept his head down. "Happens all the time."

She left the employee in the aisle and finished the rest of her shopping; stopping only to call her mother and say she'd be slightly longer than the promised twenty-minutes. The call ended up lasting much longer than Chloe had hoped when her mother instantly assumed she'd had another spell. After five minutes, Chloe was successful in convincing her mother that she was fine, just taking a little longer than she'd anticipated. She'd been tempted to tell her mother that she'd run into Dell, but decided against it in the end. She knew her mother couldn't possibly like the Blackbird's after what they'd done to Donnie. Why her mother felt the need to pretend in front of her, she had no idea, but she knew in her mother's heart, just as in her own, hatred for the Blackbird's would live eternally.

After the call, she checked out and pushed the cart to her car. The parking lot was dark when she finally popped the trunk with the remote on her key chain and began transferring her groceries. When she heard footsteps approaching, she assumed it was another shopper until Dell's voice had her turning quickly.

"Chloe, we need to talk."

"What are you doing?" she scanned the parking lot, hoping to find other shoppers near-by. There were none and panic flared to life. "Are you following me?"

Dell's dark brows pinched, "No. If you have a minute I'd like to talk to you."

She turned back to her task and worked faster moving her groceries. "I don't have anything to say to you."

"Chloe we need to talk, there's something happening and I..."

"Wait," she finished moving her groceries and slammed her trunk closed. "I do have something to say to you." She jerked the keys from her purse and stared at him. "Stay away from me." She watched as his expression darkened. His typically amber eyes now nearly black, sparked with fury. He looked dangerous and she knew she should have been afraid, but once again, she only felt safe and protected in his presence, and she hated admitting to the feeling. She didn't want to feel this way for him. *God, anyone but him!*

"We will talk Chloe. Maybe not tonight, but our confrontation *is* coming."

She gasped and stepped back, "Is that a threat?"

"No," he responded. "I am no threat to you Chloe."

She eyed him, letting her eyes rove his features, wishing to God she could see the truth of his words. Instead, she turned from him, got in her car, and drove away. She watched in the rearview mirror as he disappeared from sight.

***

Dell stood alone in the parking lot cursing himself as he watch the rear lights of Chloe's car slowly dim from sight. *Our confrontation is coming!* He admonished himself. It did sound like a threat. *What in the hell was I thinking?*

For some reason his logic seemed to fly out the window when he was around her. He couldn't explain it and it certainly wasn't his typical behavior. He wondered if his elevated Alpha status wasn't having some adverse effect on his brain.

She'd asked if he'd been following her, and he'd denied it but that had been a lie. He had been following her. He'd been outside her house all day, circling it to spy on her from whatever window gave him the best vantage point. When she'd taken out the trash earlier, he'd considered approaching her, but knew he'd have no way of explaining his presence. Finally, when she'd gotten in her car, he'd shifted and followed her to the market.

He'd run through the town in his wolf form, which was asinine. He'd have killed any member of his pack that had done anything so foolish. If anyone called the authorities, he could've been shot. It was an incredibly stupid move, but one he couldn't prevent himself from making. He had to follow her, needed to talk to her, hoped to touch her. Instead, he'd outright threatened her.

After he'd made the mistake he'd expected to scent her fear. He hadn't, but he had scented something else, something new. He'd been around her enough to know her scent. Hell, it was all he ever thought about, but it had been different this time, only slightly, not enough that any other shifter would have noticed, but he had. His lips quirked, it had been female interest. It was often emitted by the females of his kind when they wanted to be pursued.

Chapter 8

Sleep eluded Chloe again that night. 'Our confrontation is coming'. The words played over and over as she tried to decipher their meaning. While the implications were terrifying, she was slightly relieved that Dell too had realized that something strange was happening between them. She couldn't explain her sudden fainting spells when he touched her and that odd warm sensation that washed over her whenever she was in his presence. For the first time, she actually entertained the idea that he might actually be a shifter and that her reaction to him had something to do with the fact. "Great! Now I'm buying into their bullshit."

The remainder of the night was spent tossing and turning and thinking of Dell and for the following week, the days passed at an agonizingly slow pace.

Chloe had taken all her vacation at once, knowing that her mother would need her for as long as Chloe could afford to be away from the office. She truly didn't mind missing work. As an investigator for the state's child support enforcement division her job was as monotonous as it was draining. She'd accepted the position with great enthusiasm. She'd had high hopes of doing work that mattered. Unfortunately, her heart just wasn't in the work but it paid well and offered sick leave and vacation. Between both Chloe was able to take two-weeks off to spend with her mourning mother.

She and her mother had spent the first week entertaining the stream of visitors that stopped by with cards or flowers. Donnie had been well known and even more well-liked. The townsfolk, like the family, were still having great difficulty coming to terms with the fact that he was gone.

When the second week came, Chloe preoccupied herself with cleaning her mother's home, preparing meals, and helping her mother come to terms with the loss of her son.

She awoke one morning to find Bea fully dressed and sneaking out the door. She confronted her mother.

"Mom! Where are you going?"

"To work."

"Work? I hardly think you're ready."

Her mother turned a frown on her, "I *hardly* think you're qualified to offer up such an opinion."

Still in her pajama bottoms and a loose t-shirt, Chloe attempted to smooth down her disheveled hair. "You took two weeks off. You still have a few days. Why are you rushing this?"

Bea reached around to lock the door from the inside, her car keys jangling in her palm. "Because when you get to be my age you have to keep your mind pre-occupied." She took a step out the door.

"Mom!"

Bea halted, her shoulders sinking as she stared up at Chloe in resignation. "I've gotta keep moving baby. If I stall out now, I'll never get re-started."

Chloe recognized the vulnerable truth in her mother's words. She dropped down to sit on one of the carpeted stairs, her own shoulders slumping as the fight left her. "You sure?"

Bea smiled, "I'm sure." She eyed Chloe then, "Maybe just a few half days to start." She eyed her watch impatiently, "Call me around noon, we'll have lunch."

Chloe stood to quickly descend the stairs and place a warm kiss on her mother's cheek. "Lunch. Noon. Got it."

Then her mother smiled and left for work leaving Chloe standing in the doorway wondering if she too shouldn't cut short her leave and return to the office.

Fuck that! I've got vacation days and I'm gonna use 'em.

Now that she didn't have to make breakfast for her mother, and not hungry herself, she bounded back up the stairs to throw on her freshly washed running gear.

Ten minutes later, she stepped into the woods. She opted to keep her I-pod in her pocket this time. Hoping that if she paid more attention, no wildlife would sneak up on her.

She didn't push a full on run, but settled on a steady jog. Thirty minutes in she'd broken a sweat and slowed to a walk.

She heard the crunch of pine needles behind her and turned to eye the forest. Seeing nothing, but feeling slightly spooked she faced forward and resumed her jog.

Movement in the corner of her eye had her stopping. *Red fur?* She focused and saw the movement again, verifying that it was in fact red fur. *Fox.* Too small to be any real threat, Chloe ignored the fox and continued her jog, but after a few moments she noted that it was shadowing her.

She wasn't some fanatical animal rights activist, but she did believe in not disturbing an animal in its own habitat. She veered left, hoping to leave the fox to its portion of the woods. She jogged a few minutes and didn't spot the animal. Satisfied that she'd left it undisturbed she focused on her jog when she caught sight of the red fur again. Still on her right, the animal was a little closer. She ventured further left and jogged a little faster.

Unfortunately, the fox seemed determined to shadow her. It pressed closer, forcing Chloe to go further off the path than was comfortable. She wasn't familiar with this portion of the woods and knew she could easily get turned around, yet she figured a few more minutes of jogging then she'd turn and head back.

She was just about to stall out and turn to head back to town when the fox crashed through the brush and lunged at her. Shock tore through her when she realized it wasn't a fox at all. It was a small red wolf.

The wolf nipped at her heels, forcing Chloe into a dead run. She looked back and saw the wolf giving chase.

Shit! This wolf was nothing like the other she'd encountered. While smaller, it was more threatening. There was no calm serenity washing over her when she looked in its eyes, instead terror lanced through her when the wolf lunged at her feet.

Chloe jumped and sprinted faster. She had no idea where she was heading, but pushed harder. She jumped downed logs and was slapped by more than a few branches as she ducked and raced through the foliage.

She checked behind her again and the wolf was still there. It appeared to be restraining itself from attacking her. She knew it could outrun her and couldn't understand why it didn't take her down.

She crashed through a clearing and faced forward just in time to throw her body to the ground. She slid a few feet along the dewy grass as both arms snaked out and clawed into earth. She twisted her body until she was on her belly and kicked at the ground with her feet as she continued to slide toward a cliff that dropped God only knew how far.

Her hand snagged a tree root and her body was jolted to jarring halt. Pain tore through her shoulder as it bore the brunt of the full force of her weight jerking to a standstill.

Instantly, her eyes turned to find the red wolf, but it was gone. Her breath sawed back and forth and her body shook from exertion as realization slowly dawned. She pulled back her left foot, horrified that it hung just over the cliff that very nearly just killed her.

She forced herself to a sitting position, her hand reaching up to cradle her throbbing shoulder. She stood on trembling legs and tip-toed to peer over the ledge of the cliff from where she stood. She couldn't see the bottom and the revelation had her belly convulsing. She dropped to her hands and knees and coughed as her body tried to wretch. She didn't have anything to eat or drink that morning so there was nothing for her to throw up, so she dry heaved a few moments until the wave of nausea passed.

Shakily, she got to her feet and took a tentative step towards the tree line. She kept her eyes intently focused searching for any sign of the wolf. When there was none, she dropped her arms and broke into a dead run, heading back down the mountain toward home. *I am so done running in these woods!*

Back home, she showered and debated calling her friend Eden who worked for the local Fish, Wildlife, and Parks department. She'd been sure the wolf was stalking her, and if she didn't know any better she'd have actually thought the wolf was forcing her to run in the direction of the cliff.

She considered explaining the story to Eden then decided it sounded so foolish that she didn't want the embarrassment. She didn't mention it to her mother either when they met for lunch.

Chapter 9

Later that evening Chloe was going stir crazy. She'd cleaned her mother's entire house and then with nothing else to do, she cleaned in again. She'd cooked dinner, fed her mother and cleaned up the dishes so her mother could turn in early. She sat in front of the TV flipping through the channels quickly with the remote, not really watching the TV at all.

"Ughh, I gotta get out!" She picked up her cell off the coffee table. She hadn't talked to her best friend Marissa since the morning of the funeral and because the two were also co-workers, Chloe dialed her friend with high hopes of being distracted by work-place gossip that she'd missed over the past few days.

"Hello?" Marissa answered.

"Hey," Chloe didn't attempt to disguise the relief in her voice. "it's me. What are you doing?"

"Chloe! How are you doing?"

"Fine," she winced at the pity in her friends tone. "I'm going fucking stir crazy. You busy, wanna have a drink?" She crossed her fingers silently praying that Marissa was free.

"Hell yeah I wanna have a drink. Who's car we taking?"

Chloe smiled her relief. She could always rely on Marissa to be there when she needed her. The two had been friends for years, and Marissa's boisterous nature was the perfect compliment to Chloe's more reserved attitude. "Do you just wanna meet me at that new Irish pub on main and seventh?"

"Betcha I beat ya." Marissa hung up and Chloe smiled to herself thankful that her best friend was always there when she needed her.

She touched up her make-up, and laced on some boots before checking on her mother and sneaking out the door. She left the TV on so that if her mother woke, she'd think Chloe was still zoning out on the couch.

Fifteen minutes later she pulled her silver car into the parking lot of the Irish pub and noted that Marissa had indeed beaten her to the bar. When she entered the establishment, Marissa waved to her from where she stood at the bar. She leaned casually against it, one hip jutted out in form fitting jeans while two men hovered over her, drooling over her low cut shirt and exposed ample cleavage.

As Chloe approached, Marissa let her eyes rove her friend disapprovingly before she whispered to one of the men then stepped away to meet Chloe. "Seriously? *That's* what you're wearing?"

Chloe's brows shot up. She knew better than to be offended. "Sorry, I'm not really in the mood for male company right now."

Marissa turned her eyes and plucked a pretzel from a bowl on the bar before popping it in her mouth and shrugging one slim shoulder. She turned to Chloe and smiled broadly before winking. "More for me." Then she turned and sauntered back to her place at the bar with Chloe on her heels. "Sorry guys," Chloe heard her offer, "girl's night only."

"What?" One of the guys sounded genuinely offended. "Come on baby. Two men, two ladies, what's the problem?"

Chloe smirked, she knew Marissa was a huge fan of the opposite sex, but nothing turned her friend off more than a pushy guy. She watched as Marissa turned abruptly to the man that had remained silent. She stepped close and pressed her body into his. "Well if he's gonna pout, then I'll take *your* number."

The guy jerked his wallet out of his back pocket and yanked out a business card as he smiled and handed it to Marissa. The other guy cursed under his breath and stomped off.

"I'll call you." Marissa kissed the guy on the cheek, leaving a smudge of red lipstick on his smiling face before she turned to Chloe, "Come on, we'll grab a booth." Marissa stopped to rap her knuckles on the bar, "Celeste, two bottles of Bud light please." Then she followed Chloe to a booth by the window.

"I thought you said you haven't been here before," Chloe whispered staring at the bar tender as she grabbed the two requested bottles of beer from the cooler behind the bar.

"I haven't." Marissa smiled broadly pulling a ten-dollar bill from her sequin purse and holding it out to the approaching bartender, "But I'm a fast friend." She winked at the bartender, "Keep the change."

Chloe accepted a bottle from her friend and took a sip watching the bartender leave, "Hey big spender, you just gave her like a four dollar tip."

"Keeps 'em coming back." Marissa lifted the bottle to her lips and took a long swallow before righting the bottle, "So," she sobered, "how you doing? How's your mom?"

"Fine," Chloe took another drink of her beer. "We're both fine. I'm just..."she sighed eyeing the bar, not sure what her problem was.

"It's gonna take some time. I know you're not big on patience Chlo, but you can't force this."

"I know," she dropped her chin to her upraised palm, "I just feel...off."

"Well, your worlds been tipped. It's gonna take you a while to get right again."

"It's not just Donnie, it's..." *God, how do I talk about Dell without sounding like a narcissistic asshole?* "Do you remember Dell Blackbird from school?"

Marissa leaned forward bracing both elbows on the table and resting her folded hands under her chin. "Sure." She studied Chloe, "I saw him at Donnie's funeral. I can't believe he had the nerve to show up."

"Right?" Chloe barked. "My mom's been acting like I shouldn't have been offended by it, like it wasn't out of line. Then he showed up at her house…"

"What!" Marissa dropped her hands, "He showed up at your mother's house?" Her lip curled in derision, "That is so fucking classless." She kept her eyes on Chloe but lifted a hand and signaled the barmaid to bring two more beers. "Please tell me you put him in his place."

"I didn't have to."

"No! Your mother wouldn't!"

Chloe smiled at the mental image of her mother cursing out Dell. "No, she didn't either. When I answered the door, he got sick or something. He just fell and was holding his stomach."

The bartender set two more bottles on the table and Marissa slid her another ten without looking, "It was probably guilt eating away at his gut!" Her mouth twisted adding emphasis to her words. The bartender left Marissa's change and walked away.

"I don't know what it was but," she stopped to stare at Marissa unsure how much she wanted to divulge.

"Oh don't you fucking dare look at *me* that way. You know I'm good for it. Spill!"

She smiled then it faltered as she lowered her voice and took a healthy drink of her beer. "Then I ran into him again at the grocery store." She blushed, "It was so fucking embarrassing!"

"Why? What happened?"

"Honestly, I still have no idea. He was talking to my mom when I found her and I was going to hide, but I'd already been seen. When I shook his hand....Christ, I don't know if it was anger or exhaustion or what, but I..." her cheeks grew redder, "I passed out."

"WHAT!" Marissa shrieked drawing the attention of half the bar as she burst into laughter and grabbed her temples, "You passed out?"

Chloe started laughing at her friend's reaction, "God shut up!" She eyed the bar, "Everyone is staring."

"Fuck 'em!" Marissa had Chloe pinned with her gaze, "So come on," she motioned rapidly with her hands for Chloe to continue, "did you hit the floor, did you fall on your face, did you…" Marissa rose up out of her seat and curled her feet underneath her in giddy anticipation, "Oh God, please tell me you didn't land on Dell!"

"Worse!" Chloe moaned.

"WORSE?" Marissa shrieked again and inched closer to Chloe snatching her hands up into her own, "What? Tell me, I'm dying to know!"

Chloe eyed her friend over her bottle after she jerked a hand free to finish it off before wiping her lips with the back of one hand, "He caught me and carried me to my mom's car."

Marissa's eyes widened and her jaw fell open, "Are you shitting me?"

Chloe shook her head.

"Not for nothing Chloe, but he is one fine, and I do mean *fine*, piece of ass." Marissa threw back her head and laughed throatily. "That is fucking great!"

"It's not funny Marissa!" Chloe pouted, "It was humiliating. I'm supposed to be hating the guy and there he was catching me and carrying me around the damn supermarket parking lot for the whole town to see. Then when I saw him again..."

"Wait!" Marissa held up a hand. "You saw him again?"

Chloe nodded.

Marissa still had her hand up when she turned to find the bartender and shouted across the room, "Celeste, we're gonna need some shots!"

Rolling her eyes, Chloe shook her head at her friend. Good 'ol Marissa, she could always rely on her friend to make a mountain out of a mole hill. She smiled. Marissa may have been a bit of an exaggerator, but it was nice to finally talk freely about what was going on in her life.

When Celeste returned with two shots, both Marissa and Chloe picked up the glasses and eyed each other silently before downing the dark liquid without even knowing what it was. The amber concoction burned and Chloe coughed and sputtered, barely catching Marissa's order of two more shots and two more beers as she placed a twenty on the bartenders drink tray.

"Okay," Marissa took a deep breath ready to continue, "now when *exactly* did you see him again, and what *exactly* happened that time?"

Still disgusted from the foul tasting shot, Chloe took a drink of her beer and swished it around her mouth before she spoke. "Needless to say, we didn't get any shopping done, so I went back to the market the following day. I was in the frozen food section and he came up and wanted to talk."

"About what?"

Shrugging, Chloe took another sip and realized she was getting buzzed, "I have no idea. I walked away when he tried to touch me."

"Touch you where?" Marissa's eyes widened and she smiled perversely.

"Not like *that!* He tried to grab my arm."

Marissa fell back against the cushion of the booth staring whimsically over Chloe's head, "I'd *so* let him touch me anywhere he wanted."

"Marissa!"

"What? The guy's a fucking God."

"*Anyway,* he followed me out to the parking lot and said that something was happening and we needed to talk, that our confrontation was coming." She dipped her eyes to her bottle and used a polished finger nail to start peeling the edge of the label. "He's really kind of freaking me out."

"Well what did he say was happening? What does that even mean?"

"I don't know. It's just…weird stuff's been happening around him, and I…"

Marissa cut her off, "Weird stuff like what?"

Chloe chewed on her bottom lip before blowing out a breath, "When he touches me it feels…different."

"Whoa, whoa, whoa." Marissa leaned forward, "Touches you? You said he *tried*."

"Look," Chloe eyed the bar, annoyed that the bartender wasn't back with the distraction of shots, "I don't know what's going on. I just know that things are getting weird."

Marissa screwed her face into a look of skepticism, "Well you said he spoke of a confrontation. What'd he mean by that?"

"Again, I don't know."

"You know what we should do," Marissa eyed Chloe intently; "we should get a restraining order."

Chloe laughed, "A restraining order? And what are we going to say when we file for one?" She changed her tone to sound mocking, "This man has been catching me when I faint Officer, I demand you keep him away from me!"

Marissa started laughing and was distracted when Celeste came back with their round, "Okay, you're right that'll never hold up." She took the shots off the tray and placed one in front of herself and the other in front of Chloe before she snatched the

beers off the tray and eyed the change that remained before smiling

at Celeste and pushing the tray away, "Keep it."

Alone again, Marissa took up her shot glass and clinked it

off Chloe's. "Cheers." She slammed the shot and winced.

"Maybe confrontation is code for he wants to bend you over a table

and…"

"Marissa!" Chloe felt herself blush.

"Hmm," Marissa's eyes narrowed in scrutiny, "It would

appear young lady that you aren't as opposed to that type of

confrontation as you'd like me to believe."

Waving a hand dismissively, Chloe snatched up her shot

and downed it quickly hoping to quell some of her apparent

discomfort before she chased the shot with a long swallow of beer.

Marissa smiled knowingly keeping her eyes on her friend.

"Hey, I don't blame ya! I'd let him bend me over a table any day."

She laughed loudly.

"Look, I don't want to talk about this anymore. What's up

with you? How's work?" The shift in conversation worked, and

Chloe felt herself relaxing as the topic steered from her and Dell to Marissa's monotonous work week.

Too many beers and too many hours later, Chloe peeked at her watch and cringed when she discovered it was nearly closing time. "We better go."

Marissa smiled then sighed, eyeing the bar, "You're right. Wait here. Those two goons are still at the bar. I'll get 'em to give us a ride home."

"Pass!" Chloe exclaimed standing quickly only to brace her hands on the table as she swayed. "I'll get myself home." She watched as Marissa pulled lipstick and a pocket mirror from her purse and re-did her lips before smacking them together.

"Fine," Marissa hauled herself up and turned glossy eyes to the bar. "I'll take 'em both." She erupted into a peel of laughter.

"Marissa, maybe you should just go home. I can drop you off or call you a cab?"

"Why on God's green earth would I want to go home alone when there are two viable and willing specimens at the bar," she crooked a finger to beckon the two men who'd been watching her since she rose, "who are eager to satisfy my needs."

Fear sobered Chloe momentarily. "You don't know them."

The men approached and Marissa eased herself out of the booth, stopping to loop an arm through one of each man as they stood on either side of her before she winked and licked her lips devilishly, "*They* don't know me."

Ignoring the two men Chloe grabbed Marissa's shoulder, "You sure you wanna do this?"

One of the guys grabbed Chloe's elbow and jerked her into his chest, "Come on baby, you can come too."

Chloe pulled back, "I don't think so."

Marissa giggled and slapped the guy on the arm, "Leave her alone, she's not as…adventurous."

Quickly grabbing her purse, Chloe turned imploring eyes to Marissa, "We could go have breakfast, head back to my apartment. You could stay with me."

Marissa shook her head, "Don't worry about me." She pulled tighter on the two men on either side of her and smiled, "I'm exactly where I want to be."

She knew from past experience that taking two guys home wasn't anything new for Marissa, but it still left Chloe feeling like a worthless friend when the trio stumbled out the front door and out of sight. Celeste approached and was picking up the numerous empty bottles and shot glasses that littered their table when Chloe asked, "Do you know those guys?"

Celeste shrugged, "Sure. Well the one anyway. His name is Hank, he's a metal worker. He's a good guy, don't worry. He wouldn't hurt your friend."

"What about the other guy?" Chloe eyed the door nervously.

"The grabber? Not sure, just heard Hank call him Mitchell. Tonight's the first night I've seen him. But Hank's a straight arrow. Tough as nails too, he won't let Mitchell rough-up your friend."

The revelation while meant to be comforting had the opposite effect. "Thanks." Chloe hurried out the door, hoping to find Marissa still in the parking lot. She wasn't, but Mitchell was.

Chapter 10

Chloe quickly changed course and jerked the keys out of her purse as she dropped her eyes and headed for her car.

"Hey!" she heard Mitchell yell. "You're friend and Hank ditched me."

She walked faster, fingering the key to her ignition as she hit the auto button that unlocked the doors. Her heart rate kicked up when she heard the unmistakable sound of shoe leather slapping on the concrete indicating that Mitchell was running towards her.

"Hey pretty lady, wait."

She was almost to her car when Mitchell grabbed her arm and spun her to him. He grabbed both elbows and pulled her body into his as he breathed foul air down on her. "Where you going?"

"Home. Let me go!" she tried to pull from his grip, but he only held her tighter, sliding his arms to wrap them around her body.

"I heard you tell your friend that we could go to your apartment."

"I meant me and her." Chloe frowned up at the taller man, "Let me go. You're drunk."

He leaned closer, "Don't be like that."

Having had enough, Chloe shoved at him and tried to jerk free. She'd grown up with an older brother, and had learned at an early age to defend herself against a larger male. "Get your fucking hands off me!"

His hold didn't break and Mitchell just laughed, "Fucking hands?" He leaned down to whisper loudly in her ear, "That gives me an idea."

Chloe's anger quickly turned to terror when she realized the asshole wasn't going to let her go. She fumbled with her keys in one hand until she found the button she was looking for. She'd fight him if she had to but hoped scaring him off would be more effective. She hit the panic mode and the horn began to blare repeatedly while the lights flashed on and off.

Mitchell loosened his grip to cover his ears, "Hey, shut it off!"

Chloe shoved at his chest putting some space between them and turned to race for her car. She didn't make it. Strong arms wrapped around her and pulled her to him as he grabbed her wrists and wrestled her for the car keys. When he got them from her, he hit the panic button again and the horn stopped. She was on the verge of screaming when a familiar voice stopped her.

"Let her go!"

Mitchell spun with Chloe still trapped in his arms to frown across the parking lot at Dell. "Mind your own business buddy. She's with me."

Relief washed over Chloe, and she struggled to free herself from Mitchell's arms. "Let me go!"

Dell's angry eyes slid from Mitchell to Chloe then back. "Release her!" He dipped his head and glared at the other man before warning, "I won't tell you again."

Mitchell tightened his grip and laughed. It was the last sound he made.

One second Chloe was shoving against his vice-like grip and the next she was on the ground. She rolled in the gravel parking lot, snatched up her keys that were knocked a few feet away then rolled again when she heard a strange gasping sound. Her eyes locked on Dell as he crouched over Mitchell. One large hand was clamped around Mitchell's throat and the drunken man's eyes bulged in his blue face as he clawed at Dell's hand.

Chloe scrambled to her feet, "Dell, stop!" She barely recognized him for the rage that was registered on his face. His eyes were darker, his bone structure seemed more pronounced, and there was no way she could miss the deep snarl that emitted from his lips. Her eyes flashed to Mitchell, who was gulping at the air but was no longer making any sound. "Jesus Dell, you're killing him. STOP!" She reached down and pulled on his shoulder. She didn't expect the vicious snarl as Dell partially lunged at her while keeping his hand firmly locked on Mitchell's throat. Startled, she jumped back and landed on her ass when she failed to catch herself. Her mouth was open and she scrambled away from Dell as fear rushed forward.

Seeming to notice her reaction, Dell's features relaxed and he slowly turned his sneer from Chloe to Mitchell as he carefully released his grip.

Mitchell sucked in a long gasp as tears slid down his cheeks, and when Dell slowly stood lifting his weight off the other man, Mitchell rolled coughing and sputtering as he fought to fill his starved lungs.

"If you ever touch her again, I'll fucking kill you."

The words were spoken so calmly that Chloe simply stared at Dell in shock. When he approached, she fought the instinct to crawl backward. He looked different now, like the Dell she knew. His features had returned to normal and now in comparison she realized just how scary he'd actually appeared in his anger.

He approached then squatted so they were eye level. "I'm sorry I frightened you. Are you okay?"

Unable to find her voice, she simply nodded.

"Did he hurt you?"

She shook her head and lifted a hand to brush back some hair that had fallen free of her ponytail. She stilled when she heard

Dell growl. He wasn't looking at her, but at her hand. She pulled

it down to study it only to realize she was bleeding. *I must have*

cut myself when I fell. When she looked up again Dell was

standing and turned back to Mitchell. She heard him growl again

and when she peered around his legs she saw that Mitchell was

gone.

"Let me help you." Dell held out a hand, but she knew

better than to accept it.

Still convinced that he'd done something to her when he

touched her at the supermarket, she eyed his hand nervously before

she inched backward and slowly stood. She fought a wince as she

pushed up off her bleeding palms. "I'm fine thanks." Standing she

looked down at her hands and picked out a few pebbles that had

been imbedded there.

"Boyfriend of yours?"

She didn't miss the anger in Dell's tone, and couldn't

understand its source. "Obviously not!"

"So you were just going to take him home and he got out of

hand?"

She knew she was supposed to be grateful, but his low opinion of her prevented her lips from staying closed. She dropped her hands. "Fuck you, I'm not like that!"

Dell took a deep breath. "Come on, I'll give you a ride home."

Palming her keys, Chloe eyed her car. "I'm good, but thanks for the offer." She made to turn but Dell caught the sleeve of her shirt.

"You're drunk Chloe, and I'm not asking." He pulled and she had to turn to keep from falling as he led her back toward the bar.

"I am *not* drunk!" she argued, while noting that she was feeling a little queasy. She shouldn't have had so many shots. *Damn Marissa!* She tried to pull free of his grip but nearly tripped over the curb.

Dell stopped walking to frown at her, "Shall I carry you?"

The threat was there. He knew she feared his touch and was using it to force her compliance. She looked down at her keys and hit the button that locked her doors. The horn sounded once

and she frowned up at him, shrugging off his hand. "I can walk."
She pinned her eyes on the lone black truck that sat parked in front
of the bar.

When he released her shirt, he crossed to the passenger side
door and held it open.

She used the stirrup to help her climb in, but nearly lost her
balance. She was drunker than she thought. Dell's firm hand on
her ass had her tensing before she climbed into the seat then
ignored him as he closed the truck door.

"Your mother's I presume?" He started the truck and pulled
away from the curb.

She desperately wanted to go to her own apartment, but
remembered that she'd left her mother's TV on. She didn't want
Bea to wake only to discover that her daughter had snuck out. Not
to mention that for some odd reason, she also didn't want Dell to
know where she lived. "Yes."

He turned to frown at her then put his eyes back on the
road, "What were you doing with him?"

"I wasn't with *him*. I met my friend Marissa out and she just left with his friend. Apparently he thought it was an invitation."

"Well if you didn't dress like that, it wouldn't invite trouble."

Her mouth fell open as she dropped her head to eye her attire. She still wore the clothes she'd dressed in that morning to clean house. "I'm wearing jeans and a t-shirt," she ground out in incredulity.

Dell snorted.

"Well what are *you* doing out so late? Trying to find a chippy?" She hated that instead of sounding condescending she sounded jealous.

"Luckily for you I was down the road at the Hunt Inn having a beer with my pa...my friends," he amended.

"So it's okay for you to drink and drive, but not me?"

"*I'm* not drunk."

"Neither am I!" The longer she sat though, the more the effects of the alcohol were taking their toll. She desperately needed a glass of water, a handful of aspirin, and a bed.

"And I wasn't just attacked by some drunk trying to rape me."

To that Chloe didn't respond. She was just realizing how serious the situation had been and how much worse it would have been if Dell hadn't shown up.

The silence in the truck stretched a few miles before Chloe finally wrapped her arms around her waist and offered, "Thanks for saving me."

Dell looked at her and misunderstood her posture. He flipped on the heat and mumbled, "You're welcome."

She turned to frown out the window, "Must be nice to be a big guy. You can go out and have a drink with your friends anytime without having to worry about being attacked."

"Why wasn't your boyfriend with you? He should take better care of you."

She dropped her head to pick at the blood that was crusting on her palm. "I don't have a boyfriend."

"Why?"

"I don't know," she snapped. "Do you have a girlfriend?"

"No."

"Why?" she challenged.

He smiled, "I haven't yet found what I'm looking for." He turned to her, his eyes dipping to her chest then back up.

She felt her cheeks warm and turned to look out the window.

"Here," he brushed her knee and she felt a slight jolt of electricity shoot from her knee to course through her body as he leaned over and popped the glove box. He pulled out a couple of kerchiefs and handed them to her. "They're clean. Use 'em to wrap your hands."

Accepting the kerchiefs, her eyes snagged on his forearm. Three bands of slightly varying sizes were tattooed around the widest part of his forearm. She remembered the tattoos. The school had been abuzz when he'd shown up with them in high school. His sister and his brothers shared the same mark. She wondered if all his family wore the bands.

The truck was silent again and whether it was from the alcohol or his proximity, Chloe tensed and turned watching the world race by as she fought back tears. "I don't want to hate your family Dell."

He didn't respond at first and she wondered if he'd even heard her. "I don't want you to either."

"My mother loved Donnie very much. So did I."

"We loved Mace in equal measure. But…"

When he failed to continue she turned to frown at him.

"The sins of our brothers are no reflection on us Chloe."

"Us as in you and your family, or us as in you and I?"

He looked at her. "You and I."

Anger flared to life. *Donnie hadn't sinned. He was just trying to protect what was his!* "If Mace had stayed away from Beverly, everything would've been fine."

"You don't understand."

The truck pulled to a halt in front of her mother's house. "Well make me understand." She spun on him, "Explain it so that my little brain can understand why Mace wasn't in the wrong. Why it's okay to sleep with another man's wife. Why it's okay to kill him over something that is rightfully his!"

"It's complicated."

Chloe reached down and jerked on the door handle, "It's not really. You're brother took what belonged to mine, and now they're both dead for it." She climbed down from the truck and turned to glare up at him, "Pretty fucking simple to me!" She slammed the door and walked as straight as she could to her mother's front door.

***

"Fuck!" Dell growled as he ground the steering wheel between his two hands and watched Chloe disappear into her mother's house. She'd extended an olive branch, and he'd screwed it up. *I should've just kept my fucking mouth shut!*

His night had gone from bad to worse as it had progressed. First, he'd met his pack mates at the bar to watch some MMA. He knew it was a bad idea from the jump. It didn't take much for drunken men watching fights to think they all were suddenly scrappers too. He and his pack had been asked to leave after Briggs had beaten three men into oblivion. Dell had simply watched, enjoying the spectacle, but that didn't prevent the owner from eighty-sixing him as well.

Then, driving home, he'd seen Chloe exiting the new Irish pub. He'd pulled to a stop to watch her when that man had attacked her. His grip tightened on the steering wheel and it creaked under the pressure as he remembered the terror on her face. Even now, his wolf stirred at the memory.

He eyed the house one last time before turning and heading home. A few blocks from her house, Dell snatched up the bloody kerchiefs she'd left on the passenger seat and tossed them out his window. For some reason, the scent of her blood had his boiling. He kept playing over and over the sight of the man grabbing her from behind and the fear on her face. He took deep calming breaths in an attempt to soothe his wolf. *Nothing even happened,* he chastised himself. But both he and his wolf knew that had he not shown up, things could have been very bad.

"What is she even doing out this late?" His angry eyes flashed to the rearview mirror, but her house was no longer in sight. He didn't know this friend of hers, but decided instantly that she wasn't a good one if she was willing to leave Chloe alone at a bar at, his eyes flashed to the clock on his dash, nearly two o'clock in the morning! A growl rumbled from his lips and because he was alone, he didn't try to stop it.

She said she doesn't want to hate my family. God, why didn't I just stay quiet! He frowned at the dark highway, *I should've said, 'Then don't.'* His growl grew louder, *Why didn't I think of that then?*

He remembered the way she'd avoided his touch when he'd tried to help her up. It was actually painful for him the few times he'd touched her and he wondered if she'd felt it too. *Or is she avoiding touching me because she hates me?* Maybe it was the medicine she was using on him. Hell, he didn't know what her problem was.

He tried to force himself from thinking of her, but his wolf was awake and ready to fight, and Dell knew beyond a shadow of a doubt that he was in for one long sleepless night. He already thought about her too much, and with every encounter his desire for her grew. *Desire?!* He reached up and punched the dash when he realized that desire is exactly what he felt.

Chapter 11

"Not Briggs. Have Pony do it," Dell snapped impatiently causing Stevie to jump.

Pony, a cousin of Dell and Briggs was mated to Stevie. Both were shifters and both were strongly tied to the pack.

Cindy smiled apologetically at Stevie who looked on the verge of tears. "It's alright Stevie. I'll take care of it."

Stevie nodded once before rushing from Dell's office.

Cindy had been running interference for Dell's cranky attitude for the past nine days. Unfortunately, his outlook only seemed to be worsening.

"You didn't have to bark at her."

"I didn't bark," he growled without looking up from the paperwork at his desk.

"You're right. It was more of a snarl."

"Cindy..." Dell cautioned.

She eyed him, wondering if he'd thought about Chloe at all over the past several days. She was dying to know, but was unwilling to broach the subject lest it remind him of what she was hoping he'd forget. "Michael and I were wondering if you'd like to join us for dinner on Saturday."

Dell didn't stop working, "No."

"You don't even know where we're going."

"And I don't care. I still remember the last time I joined you two for dinner."

Cindy grabbed her chest in feigned shock, "Brother," she gasped, "are you implying that you did not enjoy yourself?"

"I'm not implying anything," there was humor in his tone, "I'm flat out telling you."

"She wasn't that bad," Cindy challenged.

Dell shook his head with a wince, "She was. No more blind dates."

"It doesn't hurt anything to at least date. Have a one night fling. Get laid."

He frowned up at his sister offering a sarcastic, "Nice."

"Well!" She jabbed a finger towards him, "You're going to need to start looking. It's not good to have a mate-less Alpha."

"It's dangerous to have a mated one," he countered.

"That's so archaic and you know it. No one would dare challenge you let alone try to harm your mate to hurt the pack. It hasn't happened in…I can't even remember the last time it occurred."

Dell slammed down his pen, "Has it escaped you that I'm trying to work here?"

Cindy wordlessly grabbed a stack of paperwork from his desk when her ears picked up an approaching vehicle. She tensed and her eyes flicked to Dell who was already halfway to the window.

"Finally!" he rumbled turning quickly. "Mama's home."

Shit! She chased quickly on Dell's heels as he strode quickly down the long hall, through the kitchen, then out the back door.

Mama's cherub-like cheeks glowed with a pink hue as she smiled her greeting. She had just gotten out of her SUV when her feet stuttered to a halt and her smile faded. She lifted her head and took a slow breath in through her nose. "What's wrong?"

Cindy rushed out the back door and slammed into Dell's back shouting over his shoulder, "Nothing! Welcome back. How was it? Is Aunty Connie doing well?"

Mama ignored her and frowned up at Dell, "What's wrong?" she demanded.

"We need to talk." Dell took her bag and ushered her inside.

Mama led the way heading straight for the office, not even bothering to remove her coat. Inside she turned and eyed Dell anxiously, "Well?"

Dell approached and grabbed her coat, helping her ease her arms from the sleeves before he folded it over the back of a chair and extended his arm indicating that she should sit. He knew she'd refuse if he didn't start talking. "What do you know of the Lott family?"

"I know much," she pursed her lips frowning up at Dell as she took a seat, "be more specific."

Once Mama sat Dell crossed to lean on the edge of his desk, crossing his thick arms across his chest. "Are they medicine people?"

Mama frowned, "No."

"Do they have ties to medicine people?"

Cindy, who'd been standing silently by the door interrupted, "Dell we shouldn't bother Mama with this now, she's exhausted." Cindy smiled tensely at her mother, "Don't you want to take a nap?"

Mama frowned at Cindy, knowing she was trying to be a distraction. "Son, what's going on?"

Dell sighed and dropped his arms, turning to frown out the window. "I think Chloe Lott has been using medicine on me."

Mama's eyes widened and she slowly stood pointing a finger at Cindy.

"Mama!" Cindy hissed, "It'll only end badly. Think of Mace."

"It's not your place to decide young lady!" Mama shook her finger at Cindy and turned then grabbing her son's hand.

"Dell, Chloe isn't using magic on you son. She's done nothing wrong."

Dell could sense his mother's fear that he'd harm Chloe for what she'd done to him. "I don't want to hurt her." Dell's tone was accusatory.

Mama grinned, "Of course you don't, nor could you. It'd be impossible for you to harm your most valued gift."

His brows knitted, "Valued gift? What in the hell are you talking about?"

"Don't!" Cindy tried to intervene but only succeeded in earning herself disapproving frowns from both Mama and Dell.

When she looked back to Dell, Mama's eyes lit with a fire as her lips spread in wide smile, "Son, she's your mate."

Taking a step back, he visibly paled. "What? You're wrong."

"I'm not wrong. If you stop and listen for a moment, you'll feel her." Mama lifted a fragile knuckle to rap it on Dell's solid chest just above his heart. "Right there. Still yourself son."

Mama leaned closer and closed her eyes with a smile. "Listen. Do you feel her?"

Dell didn't still. He stepped away from his mother's touch. "It's medicine. She's fooling you."

Mama's eyes flew open and her cheeks flamed with indignation, "If anyone's the fool here it's you." Then she jabbed a finger in Cindy's direction. "Her too. She's been lying to you to protect you."

Dell turned a scowl on his sister. "It's forbidden. A pack member cannot intentionally deceive their Alpha."

In response Cindy dipped her head. "I would gladly take the punishment for such offense if it kept you from harm."

"You admit it?" Dell challenged.

Her words were strong with conviction, "I deceived my Alpha to protect my brother." She held his gaze and jutted her chin defiantly, "I'd do it again."

Dell stood frowning at her, unsure how to react. He could punish her.

"Son, what matters here is what is happening to you. *For you*. You've been gifted with your mate. You need to claim her."

"Claim her? I can't claim her." He turned and stomped to the window leaning heavily on the sill. "She hates us. All of us, most especially me!"

"She'll forgive you..."

"No! She won't." He stood and shoved an angry hand into his hair. "We're not discussing this. She is not my mate and there will be no claiming."

Mama tensed. "Your wolf has decided. It cannot be undone. It is impossible."

"Nothing is impossible!" Dell growled furiously turning to scowl at Mama. "*I* am the Alpha and I'll decide my own fate. I am finished discussing this, it's not to be addressed again."

Anger flared to life high on Cindy's cheeks and she moved to stand behind Mama, placing a hand reassuringly on her mother's shoulder.

Mama spoke calmly, "Mace was supposed to live a long and full life. We all thought this. You refused to learn our stories, learn our rituals because you assumed you didn't need to. Like the rest of us you assumed he'd always be there. Now, you need to know. Once a mate has been chosen, your wolf will not deny her. It will become more and more painful for you the longer you keep from her. Until then it'll be just as physically painful for you to touch her. You will not be allowed to have her until you're prepared to accept her as your mate. We are designed this way so you can't try to get her out of your system. She'll not leave your thoughts son, you can't out run her."

"Enough!" Dell commanded angrily.

"Whoa, what's going on?" Briggs stopped with the door to the office half opened as he eyed first Dell then his mother and sister.

"Nothing!" Dell snapped.

Briggs stepped back to allow his brother to stomp past.

Briggs turned to his mother. "What did I miss?"

***

Having quickly been apprised of the situation, Briggs raced out of the house to catch up with Dell. As he typically did when he was stressed, Dell had stomped off into the forest.

When Briggs finally caught up to him he said nothing, but simply kept pace at his brother's side.

"I think your mother's senile!"

Briggs smiled. He knew Dell would talk if he was just given time. "*My* mother?" he scoffed. "How come every time she says or does something you don't agree with she becomes *my* mother?"

Dell snorted, a light smile lifting a corner of his mouth. "Because I find it hard to believe that any relation of mine would believe something so idiotic."

Briggs tried to hide his smile. "You know she's been around long enough to know what she's talking about here right?"

Dell growled, "It can't work!"

"How do you know?"

"How do I know?" Dell spun on his brother in incredulity grabbing both of his arms roughly, "We killed her brother and she fucking hates me! That's how I know!"

"First of all, we didn't kill her brother. Second, give her some credit. She might not hold a grudge."

Dell rolled his eyes and shoved Briggs back. "Clearly, you haven't met her."

Briggs shrugged, "I could seek her out."

Dell stopped. The flash of jealousy that shot through him felt like a punch to the gut. "Don't!" he growled the warning.

"I'll just have a talk with her," Briggs feet halted when Dell pulled to a standstill, "if she's not agreeable to a meeting with you, I'll just throw her in the trunk and haul her ass up here."

Dell knew Briggs was baiting him, trying to draw him into a physical confrontation. The three brothers had done it for each other often over the years. When one was stressed or under great pressure the other two volunteered as punching bags. Now though was the first time Mace wouldn't be present, and his absence hurt. Compounding matters was the fact that Dell didn't want to just hurt Briggs for threatening Chloe; he wanted to literally rip him apart. The swell of violence was startling and Dell couldn't help but wonder if there was something to the mating thing between him and Chloe after all.

"Don't talk about her Briggs. It angers me."

"Good," Briggs punched Dell in the bicep, "that's what I was trying for. You need to get out some stress." Briggs reached up and pushed Dell hard in the chest, "Let's go."

Dell dipped his head and growled menacingly, "Don't."

"Aw, what's wrong?" Briggs quickly pulled his shirt over his head and tossed it aside before kicking off his shoes, "You don't want this big bad wolf hunting your little red riding hood?"

Dell didn't move, but his hands balled into tight fists as he continued to growl. He was trying to restrain himself, as he often had, but something about the way Briggs was referencing Chloe had his blood boiling.

"You just don't want me around her because you don't want her to think I'm the better specimen." Briggs rolled his shoulders and grinned at his brother, "I am viable you know, maybe I'll just go over and *sniff* around. If I like what I scent, I'll take a little taste. Let you know if she's worth the hassle."

That was all it took. Dell launched himself at Briggs, hitting his brother solidly in the chest. The two rolled and Briggs didn't get the chance to recover before a large fist connected with his jaw. His head snapped to the side and he was surprised at the power behind it. He threw his own punch that Dell swiftly ducked.

Grabbing Brigg's extended arm, Dell fell back and trapped the arm between his legs and pulled back in what he knew had to be a painful arm-bar. It was one thing for a shifter to get his ass kicked in a fight, but to make one submit was quite an achievement. None of the three brother's had ever submitted to each other in battle, or to anyone else for that matter. It didn't stop them from trying.

Briggs howled before he shifted. Dell lost his grip and also shifted as he rolled. The brothers went at each other and fur flew. Vicious snarling rent the air and twenty minutes later the two brothers lay laughing on the forest floor. Blood trickled from Briggs' nose and Dell's lip was cracked. Each bore bruises and scratches and when Brigg's picked part of a dry leaf off his tongue the brothers erupted into laughter again.

"Christ, you like to cheat in your old age!"

"Old age?" Dell laughed, "I'm a spring chicken."

"Yeah," Briggs lifted a hand to rub his sore bicep, "a chicken at least."

Dell sat up then hauled himself to his feet before extending a hand to help his brother up. "What's wrong? Did this big bad wolf hurt more than just your body?"

Briggs frowned at his brother, but accepted his hand. "I assure you my pride is intact." He dusted leaves off himself when he stood. "Besides, I had to let you win. You're the Alpha."

Dell winked at his brother then rolled his head from side to side. "I needed that."

Briggs slapped him on the back, "Anytime."

"Same time tomorrow?" Dell challenged.

"Hell no," Briggs rubbed his lower back gingerly. "You better call Pony he's younger and has more to prove. I'm getting too old for this shit!"

The brothers both laughed as they headed back toward the compound.

Chapter 12

Chloe had just finished showering and dressed in a pair of comfortable jeans and t-shirt. She'd spent the morning at the local rec center gymnasium. While the facility was cramped and dingy, it was suitable for her needs, plus she didn't have to worry about any more wolf encounters.

She was descending the stairs when the doorbell rang. She paused at the landing wondering who could be calling. When the bell sounded again, she descended the last few steps to jerk the door open. Shock froze her in place as she stared at the woman she knew to be Dell Blackbird's mother.

Chloe simply stood and stared slack-jawed at the elderly woman before she finally found her tongue. "Uhh, forgive me." Chloe stood back holding the door wide, "Please come in."

Mama smiled but remained outside. "You know who I am?"

Chloe nodded, "Yes."

"And you know my son Dell?"

Chloe stiffened and bit out another clipped, "Yes."

"Good," the older woman's dark eyes crinkled in the corners when she smiled, "I'm too old to futz around, so I'll just say what needs to be said." She lifted her head and pursed her lips a moment before she began, "My people, my family, we're descendents of wolves. Shape shifters. Some call us skin walkers. You've heard the rumors?"

Chloe merely nodded.

"We live in packs and each pack has a leader, an Alpha, and it is this Alpha's responsibility to act in a manner that will both protect and strengthen his people."

"All due respect Mrs. Blackbird, but why are you telling me this?"

Mama sobered then, seemingly drawing to her full height, slight as it was. "Because Dell is the leader to our people. My son is Alpha to our clan. They are not rumors. We are shifters," Mama leveled her eyes on Chloe, "and you are my son's mate."

Chloe's eyes widened and she took a cautious step back, "Look, I don't want any trouble." Chloe peeked over the woman's shoulder wondering if she were alone. *This has to be a joke.* "You should go."

"I'll go, but I want you to know that his claiming is going to be stronger with you because he is the Alpha." Mama let her eyes slide up and down Chloe's lithe frame. "You must be very strong to have resisted to this point." Mama began to turn then, "But it cannot last young lady. No matter how much you pray it to the contrary, your hate will give way to love." Mama stopped to eye Chloe suspiciously, "I suspect it's begun already."

Chloe's blush was telling even as she lifted her chin with more confidence than she actually felt. "Good night Mrs. Blackbird," she offered dismissively.

The older woman smiled, "It's Mama." She winked. "Least it will be. The longer he stays from you the more painful it becomes. I thought it only fair to warn you now that he won't be able to stay away much longer." She reached out and patted Chloe's hand. "Prepare yourself. Prepare your heart. Your mate is coming for you." Then she turned and left.

Chloe waited until the old woman was out of sight before she closed the door and then fell back against it. *Shifter? Mates?* It was now official. The Blackbird's were certifiably nuts!

She lifted a hand to her lips and realized she was trembling. She'd instantly denied Mrs. Blackbird's words, but alone now she was staggered by the implications. *What if it's true? It can't be. Can it?* Even just considering that the stories were true was terrifying, but the old woman had seemed so truthful, almost proud of the fact. Still, Chloe wouldn't accept the woman's claim. If she did in fact believe that the Blackbirds were shifters then she'd have to believe the rest of their mother's statement and she had no intention of being anything with Dell Blackbird, especially his mate. She drew in a shaky breath. For some odd reason she couldn't slow her heart as it thundered in her chest as she remembered Mrs. Blackbird's warning. *'His claiming is going to be stronger with you because he's the Alpha.'* *What in the hell does that mean?*

Pushing up off the door, she rested a hand on her chest hoping to calm the fluttering beat within. She felt nauseated. *A game? But why would the mother get involved?* Chloe sobered,

because of Mace. She grew fearful then. *If they're willing to go to*

this extent just to mess with me, how far are they willing to go?

Her eyes drifted upward toward the area of ceiling that rested just

under her mother's bed. *Surely they wouldn't...* She gritted her

teeth then, "No they won't."

She ripped her jacket off the hook behind the door and

snagged her car keys before setting off for the Blackbird

compound.

She had to stop and ask for directions several times before

she found someone who knew the location of the Blackbird

compound.

As she maneuvered her car over the winding mountain

road, she cursed herself for not having traded in her car for a truck

last year as she'd intended. *Montana girl with a car, what a joke!*

She drove for endless minutes and had opted to back out of

the confrontation with Dell several times, but the road was too

narrow and with no opportunity to pull-off, she was forced to carry

on.

Several times, flashes of movement deep in the forest had her slamming on the brakes. Once she swore she caught the briefest glimpse of fur. *Bear? No, too small. Wolf?* She nearly laughed aloud even as uncertainty took hold. She remembered Mrs. Blackbird's words. '*They are not rumors. We are shifters.*'

As Chloe took her foot off the brake she prayed the old woman was senile before chastising herself. "See! This is exactly how they want you reacting."

When she finally crested a small slope she cringed as she heard the bottom of her car scrape on the earth. Her heart rate accelerated when her eyes rested on the large building that could only be the Blackbird compound.

The two-story home was massive. The walls were made of rich thin bricks that stacked high and were topped with a slopping green metal roof. The façade was dotted with several windows. The structure was long and a row of cars sat parked facing the length of the building. It was indication that many bodies resided on the premises. Toward one end of the structure a set of stairs led up to a deck that ran the length of the building. The deck area was even with several doors that would allow occupants to apparently exit their rooms without having to go through the house. Chloe turned her head and eyed an equally impressive barn that sat just opposite the house.

The grass was shorn in an acre size area that encompassed the house and barn but beyond that the plush forest grew wild and thick.

With her foot on the brake, she scanned the area searching for any movement. *No one's seen me. I can still back out.* "No!" She gripped the steering wheel tightly, "If you don't confront them now, things'll only get worse."

Chapter 13

She pulled her car to a halt next to the line of trucks, jeeps, and SUV's that lined the westerly wall of the house. When she exited the vehicle she was startled to find the woman who'd introduced herself the night of Donnie's funeral quickly approaching her.

Cindy.

"What are you doing here?" Cindy demanded.

"I'm here to speak to Dell."

"No."

Chloe slammed her car door, "I'm not leaving 'till I do."

"Yes you are…"

"CINDY!"

Both women turned to find Dell and Briggs approaching.

"But brother, she…"

"Enough!" Dell barked.

Chloe noted how the other woman was instantly silenced. When the brother's were close enough, Briggs grabbed Cindy's arm and pulled her away, "Come on."

Chloe didn't bother with preamble when her eyes locked on Dell. "I want you and your family to leave us alone."

Dell was watching her. Staring too intently. "Please come inside." He moved aside and extended a hand in invitation.

"No." she fidgeted nervously, "I just want to come to an understanding."

He tilted his head as he watched her, his nostrils flaring.

Chloe swore he leaned in marginally. *Is he smelling me?*

"It's going to rain." He kept his arm extended.

Tilting her head back to eye the sky, Chloe was about to protest his forecast when a clap of thunder sounded in the distance. She dropped her head to eye her surroundings nervously. *They could bury you in the woods and no one would ever know.*

"Chloe," his tone was soft, "I swear on my life that no one here is going to harm you."

When she looked about to cave he continued, "And you're right. We do need to talk, for the sake of both our families."

Mom. With a confidence born of concern over her mother's safety, Chloe took a tentative step and then another before Dell dropped his hand and stood back allowing her to pass.

When she nearly brushed him, he recoiled as if he'd been shocked. He recovered quickly, but not quickly enough for Chloe not to have noticed. It wasn't the first time he'd reacted in such a manner to her touch. At first it had been insulting, but now frankly, it was beginning to scare her a little.

Chloe stopped to stare at him with brows raised. "I'm not diseased."

Dell shook his head, "Of course not." He shook his head before following her back to the house.

Back inside, Dell took the lead and led Chloe through an immaculate kitchen down a long corridor and into a large office.

"Please have a seat."

She pulled off her jacket and hung it over the back of the chair before taking a seat. She expected Dell to take the seat behind the desk. Instead he took the chair directly across from her.

"What can I do for you Chloe?"

His amenable tone was grating. "I want you and your family to back off!"

"Back off?"

"Yes! Back. Off." She reached up to tuck a stray strand of hair behind her ear then wished she hadn't when Dell's eyes lingered there then slowly slid down the satiny column of her throat to rest on the pulse that beat there. She swore the path his eyes took felt like a caress. *Christ!* She prayed he couldn't see her heart rate hike as he watched her.

Dell didn't lift his eyes from her throat, "And just which members of my family are the cause of your distress?"

"Your mother came to see me."

With the revelation, Dell's eyes snapped to hers and he instantly noted that for once he didn't have to grind his teeth against the pain. *Proximity appears to be soothing.* "And what *exactly* did my mother want?"

She couldn't hide the flush that stole across her cheeks. "It's irrelevant, but I want you to call them off. All of them." She dipped her head, "I apologize for any disrespect I may have

---

exhibited, but when Donnie died..." she didn't need to finish. "I don't want any trouble." She raised her eyes to his then, "I want this to end before my mother is involved, she doesn't need to be hurt any more than she already has."

Dell sat back in his seat, his dark eyes flashing in anger. How dare his pack act so irrationally that this woman, *his* woman would have to come to him to beg for peace. He knew she would rather die than have to beg, especially of him.

"Other members of my family have harassed you as well?"

Again she averted her eyes. "Someone's been following me."

"Who," he demanded.

She shook her head, "I'm not sure. I've only seen them in the woods."

"The woods?"

"I go jogging. They've been," she shrugged a shoulder, "following me. I think they want me dead."

Dell sat straighter. His grip tightened on the arms of the chair and he had to force himself to relax when Chloe's eyes flashed to the sound of the creaking wood. "You've seen this person. What does he look like?" His gut wrenched when she caught her plump bottom lip between perfect white teeth.

"I didn't see much, it happened too quickly. Reddish fur, smaller than the first wolf."

Her nonchalance with the subject was unnerving and had him questioning whether or not it was some form of well laid trap. "Wolf? You're being followed by a wolf?"

She raised her eyes to his. She knew he needed to see the truth in her words. Hell, she couldn't understand herself why she even believed it. "I encountered a wolf about two weeks ago. He was large and approachable."

"And you encountered a second wolf?"

"Yes. It wasn't as…"

"Approachable," he supplied.

She nodded.

"Has it tried to harm you?"

"I can't say for sure."

Dell ground his teeth together. *If someone tried to hurt her*... "What do you mean you can't say? Either it has or it hasn't."

"I tried to stay away from it, leave it alone. I almost fell off a cliff in the process. I'm not certain if it was the wolf's fault or mine. It seemed to be steering me in that direction. Luckily I'm fit enough that I was able to save myself."

"And you think these wolves have something to do with my family?"

"I'm not saying they do or they don't. I'm just asking that since you're the Alpha if you could call them off, ask them to leave me and my mother alone."

"Alpha? What other stories has my mother told you?"

She shoved out of her chair then, "Look, I'm not accusing you or your *people* of anything. I'm just asking—if it is your family—for you to make them stay away."

Dell stood too, pacing slowly to put himself between her and the door. "Do you have any idea how crazy that sounds?"

She felt her cheeks flame, *Oh God, what if I was wrong.* "It's hard to believe and it's even harder to say."

"So you think I'm the Alpha to a pack of shape-shifting werewolves?"

"When you put it like that it sounds ridiculous."

"It *is* ridiculous."

Her shoulders slumped as she dropped her head and mumbled under her breath, "I knew I shouldn't have come."

"You don't find it alarming that your standing here appealing to what you think is the leader of a fictitious breed of humans?"

"I don't care what you are," she challenged angrily, "I only care how you conduct yourselves." Tears stung at the back of her eyes, "I'm here being as honest and as forthright as I can possibly be. I had hoped you'd have the fucking decency to approach this in the same manner."

When Dell laughed mockingly, she jerked her jacket up from the chair and made to leave when he intentionally blocked her path.

"Get out of my way!"

He couldn't let her go yet. This was the first time in weeks he'd been at peace. He'd have to take the chance that he could trust her.

"It was me."

She lifted stunned eyes to his.

"That first wolf in the woods, it was me."

She rolled her eyes as she shoved an arm into her sleeve, "Yeah? Ten seconds ago I'm a freak and now you wanna play along?"

She needed proof. Dell cleared his throat, "You were having a break down over Donnie."

Chloe stilled with her second arm halfway into her sleeve, letting silence hang between them for several long moments before whispering, "It was a very personal moment."

"I know."

She fought the wave of embarrassment the swamped her, "It wasn't yours to witness."

"I know and I apologize for intruding. It was unintentional. When I scented your pain…"

Her mouth opened slightly.

"I thought someone was injured."

The frown he'd been so accustomed to seeing on her soft features returned. "*Someone* was injured."

"Chloe, please sit down. We need to finish this."

She chewed on the inside of her lip before crossing her arms over her chest and reclaiming her seat. "Are you going to call them off or not?"

He followed her then sat behind the desk before he nodded once, "Yes."

"Thank you." she stood again, "Then we're finished."

"Wait."

Why did she have the strangest feeling that she should leave and leave *now*? "I have to go."

"I want to know what else my mother told you."

She cursed the telling flush that stole across her cheeks. "Nothing, just the truth about your people."

"You should know I can scent deceit."

Her eyes found his, "That must be very useful."

"It is." He slowly stood leaning forward and bracing his hands on the desk. "What else did she tell you Chloe?"

She smiled, shaking her head as she dropped her eyes to watch one small hand massage the other. "She threatened me."

"Threatened how?"

She kept her eyes down. "She said you were coming for me."

"Did she say why?"

Taking a step back she looked up, "She thinks I'm your..." she gave a weak laugh. "She thinks I'm your mate."

"And *that's* threatening to you?" he challenged.

"I don't want any trouble. I don't want my mother brought into this, and I don't want whatever it is that you are to affect my mother's life. You have no cause to hunt me."

"Mating is not hunting."

Her flush deepened. "It is for those who won't allow it."

"You're behavior here today suggests you might be agreeable to our way of life."

"I've done nothing to suggest that."

"Your apparent ease of acceptance of my people is sufficient enough in and of itself for any shifter to want to claim you."

"So my flaw is my acceptance?"

He slowly came around the desk and smiled as he dipped his head to eye her, "I didn't say it was a flaw."

Her heart rate kicked up and she wondered if he could hear it. "I don't know if there's any truth to it and I don't care. If your mother's intention was to frighten me, it worked."

He stepped closer, "It was not her intention." Still he stalked closer, "And it is true Chloe." Finally, within reach he lifted a hand and reached for her, "You *are* my mate."

"Don't touch me!" she jumped back. "Every time you touch me, something happens."

He smiled then dropping his hand, "It's because we're bound."

"No," her brows knitted, "we aren't!"

"It's funny actually. At first, when you dropped me to my knees at your mother's house, I thought you were using medicine on me. I hadn't been concerned in the least with the mating ritual so I never bothered to learn anything of it. I wasn't aware of what was actually happening."

"I didn't harm you."

He fought the smile that her honesty drew forth. "I know now that you did not, but I didn't know what was happening at first. I wasn't aware the ritual had begun."

"Ritual?"

"We don't just date and then decide to marry. Our mates are pre-destined. When we meet them..."

"Wait," she held up her hands, "I don't want to hear this. I don't want to hear any more of your family's secrets." She backed up until she hit the wall, "The less I know, the safer for everyone involved." She reached around and clicked the door open behind her, "We agree to stay away from each other, leave each other's family in peace. Thank you for that." She turned to exit the room, but his next words halted her.

"That's not what I agreed to."

She turned to eye him over her shoulder, anger sparking to life. "But you said…"

"I said I'd call off my pack, that they'd leave you and your mother in peace." He grinned, "*I* didn't agree to stay away from you."

"Why are you backing out of our deal?"

"Deal," he challenged. "A deal signifies that there has been some bargain struck. Here, only I've agreed to give you what you seek. You have yet to agree to reciprocate."

She didn't bother to disguise the incredulity in her tone. "You want me to give you something in exchange for calling your pack off my family?"

Dell let his eyes slide up and down her slight frame, noting how she shivered under his scrutiny. "Yes."

"What do you want?"

Silence hung between them and she couldn't seem to pull her eyes from his.

"Your character is as intriguing as your beauty. Pity the first can be used to manipulate you."

"What do you want?" Chloe demanded again angrily.

"You."

The simple word hung between them for several breathless moments.

"No," she yanked the door open and walked away.

"Not even for the sake of your mother?"

The words drew her to a halt. She turned her head but didn't meet his eyes as she whispered, "You'd use my mother to get what you want from me?"

He walked slowly toward her until he was towering over her, his chest a breath away from her back as he lifted his fingers to rub her satiny hair between them. "Right now, I'd use anything I could, but it's not what you think. The red wolf you described must be an outsider. None of my pack would be so foolish. If he's not one of mine you'll need our protection."

"No one else has cause to bother us."

"Until I know for sure, I'll assign a security detail to you and your mother."

"NO!" she spun on him then, "I don't want you coming closer, I want you moving further away." She threw up her hands, "Look, if you don't know who it is, it's probably just a real wolf."

"Real wolves are just as dangerous."

"I can take care of myself."

"You no longer need to."

"What does that mean?"

"It means that you coming here was the biggest mistake you could have ever made. You should have stayed away. Now, you know too much."

Her eyes grew wide. "I would never tell…"

"That's not a concern of mine." He groaned and raked a hand through his hair, "I wish you'd have never come."

Chloe jumped, her eyes shooting over her shoulder when she heard footsteps at the other end of the hall. Two large men stood, hands balled into fists, clearly prepared for battle. Her body began to tremble and she turned imploring eyes to Dell to whisper, "Wh-what are you going to do?"

He pinned her with his gaze, "I'm going to let you go home. I'm going to assign you and your mother protection. Unfortunately for you, your presence here has stirred my wolf within. He's making demands and I must comply."

She shook her head in confusion.

"I'm going to give you the opportunity to come to me of your own free will. I expect you here every Friday. Pack a bag and plan to stay until Monday."

"But. I can't..."

"*If* you fail to come to me of your own accord," he stepped closer slowly drawing in the scent of her, "then my mother's *threat* will come to fruition. Don't make me come for you Chloe, you won't like the consequences." His eyes darted to the two men at the end of the hall, "AJ, follow her home. Ensure she arrives safely. Pony! Get to the forest just south of her mother's residence. I want to know who's stalking those woods."

Chloe watched as one man disappeared and the other slowly approached as if waiting on her. When she turned back to Dell he was letting his eyes rove her features.

"I'll see you Friday. In the mean time no jogging in the woods."

For a brief moment, she thought he was going to lean down and kiss her. Instead he turned and walked back to his office.

"Dell! Why are you doing this?"

He stopped and turned back to her, "I want to see if there is in fact something to this mating bond we share." He kept his eyes on her face, "AJ, get her home."

"Wait!"

Dell ignored her plea and entered his office, closing the door firmly behind him.

Chloe turned to stare at AJ. "Is there someone else I can talk to, someone in charge?"

AJ smiled cynically, "Sorry. He's the Alpha. There's no one higher on the totem pole than that. Come on, I'll walk you to your car."

Unsure what else to do, Chloe followed AJ out and climbed into her car. She drove through the rain as quickly as she could down the mountain road that led to the highway. Unlike her arrival, she was no longer concerned with the undercarriage of her vehicle as she pushed to put some distance between herself and the Blackbird compound.

To her surprise and terror, a large gray wolf shadowed her vehicle, not even attempting to conceal itself.

AJ?

"Ridiculous! This whole fucking thing is just..." she couldn't supply a better word, "RIDICULOUS!" What in the hell had just happened. She'd gone to Dell hoping to appeal to his sense of righteousness. It was apparent now that he didn't have any. She'd feigned belief in their stupid myths and what had it gotten her? *Mated! Or claimed, or whatever the hell it was he said.*

Her fingers ached from the death-grip they had on the steering wheel. Compounding matters was the fact that she'd actually hoped to catch him slipping and prove to her that the shifter myth was just that. Instead, if anything, he'd only confirmed it. How else would he have known about her break down in the forest? *And* he scented my lie? Really? Hysterical laughter bubbled to the surface.

When her tires finally found the pavement at the end of the long dirt road, she pressed the pedal solidly to the floor in hopes of losing the wolf that was tailing her.

What do I do now? Move? The idea was insane. There was no way in hell her mother would agree to packing up and moving out of state. They had nowhere to go. *He's gotta be just messing with me.* She laughed aloud. *Of course he is. Why did I go there? To get him to tell his family to leave mine alone? Instead, he's jumped on their bandwagon. Asshole!* She was reaching and she knew it.

Chapter 14

"You did what?" Dell boomed.

Cindy lifted her chin defiantly, "I asked Hannah to keep an eye on her."

Dell took a menacing step closer, "And are you aware that Hannah nearly killed her?"

Cindy's chin dropped, her fine brows drawing together. "No."

Dell slammed a fist down on the table nearest him. He sneered at Cindy, but spoke through the pack ties so that every member of his pack would hear him. *Chloe Lott is my potential mate. Any attempts to harm her or her family are to be considered attempts against me. Such attempts are punishable by death. Should any of you try to harm her, I will exact this very punishment myself!*

Cindy's shoulders slumped. She'd fucked up and she knew it. "Hannah?" she questioned, knowing the shifter would have to be dealt with.

"She's your fucking minion," Dell ground out. "You'll have to punish her because I'd kill her right now."

She nodded once then made to leave the office.

"Cindy!" Dell barked.

She turned to eye her Alpha.

"If one of them tried to hurt Michael, what would you do?"

Cindy's jaw clenched, her eyes darkening as she balled her hands into small fists. "Understood." Then she turned and stalked out of the office.

Still tense, Dell cleared his thoughts and focused as he felt a mental nudge that signified that one of his pack were trying to communicate.

I've found sign in the woods. It was Pony. *Your stalker is Hannah.*

I know! Come home.

***

The day after her encounter with Dell, Chloe had decided to follow in her mother's footsteps and return to work early. Her mother didn't protest when she'd packed up and headed back to her own apartment. She seemed almost relieved that Chloe was finally convinced that she'd be fine on her own.

Unfortunately, even the monotony of catching up on her backlog of work did little to ease her frame of mind. By Tuesday she couldn't stop thinking about Friday. Who was she kidding? She'd been thinking about Friday since the day she'd left Dell. She didn't know what he intended when she failed to show up, but she absolutely, one hundred percent, had no intention of showing her face anywhere near the Blackbird compound.

"If you don't come to me of your own free will my mother's threat will come to fruition", she scoffed with little conviction. He'd threatened that she wouldn't like the consequences if he had to come for her, and her mind had been racing ever since trying to figure out what exactly those consequences could be. Sad part was she didn't fear him. As much as she should, she only felt completely safe with him. *Protected.* She knew he wouldn't harm her, but it was all the mating talk that had her belly in knots. First thing on Monday she'd Googled wolves to read about their mating rituals. She didn't like what she found. Wolves mated for life.

Every day at noon she stayed at her desk and ate a cold sandwich from the vending machine, too afraid to venture out of the office. She'd pulled up local private investigators on the Internet and was contemplating hiring a guy to find out all he could on the Blackbirds. Problem was she wasn't certain she wanted to go sniffing around a large family of schizos that actually thought they were werewolves.

Shifters, she corrected herself. Apparently there was a difference between the two. Werewolves were supposedly only able to shift during a full moon and could only be killed with silver bullets. Shifters on the other hand were supposedly of Native ancestry and could shift at will. She'd researched quickly, knowing the mortification she'd experience if a co-worker caught her researching such absurdities. *I can't believe they have me buying into this crap.*

"Whatcha working on?"

Chloe straightened in her chair as she realized she wasn't working on anything. She'd been gazing out the window, thinking of Dell Blackbird. "Oh," her hand snaked out and grabbed the

nearest file as her eyes quickly scanned the label, "the Williams'
case. Just taking a breather to collect my thoughts."

"Really?" Her friend and co-worker, Marissa, plopped
down in the empty chair that sat adjacent to Chloe's desk. Her
short dishwater blonde hair was cut into a sleek sexy style that
while Chloe envied, she knew she'd never be able to pull off
herself.

Marissa and Chloe had become instant friends the first day
Marissa had been hired. "Maybe you came back too soon."
Marissa's eyes were consoling. "No one would say anything if
you took another week or so."

Heat flooded Chloe's cheeks as she realized she should still
be mourning her brother rather than wasting her time and energy
thinking about Dell. "I'm fine Marissa, really."

Marissa smiled warmly, "Well what do you say we have a
drink this weekend? A girl's night out."

The prospect was actually quite appealing. "That sounds
surprisingly great."

"Good," Marissa stood slapping a hand on Chloe's desk as she smiled at her, "Saturday, seven. Meet you at the Kasbah?"

Chloe nodded as she flipped open the file, "I'll be there."

Marissa walked toward the door, "I'll call Laura and Amanda. It'll be fun."

"You don't have to sell me on it Marissa. I could use a drink more than you know."

"Oh, you'll get your drink, and then some." Marissa winked at Chloe before she left the office closing the door behind her.

When Friday finally rolled around, Chloe was a bundle of nerves. She couldn't concentrate on anything for longer than ten seconds and every time her door opened or her phone rang, the unexpected interruption set her nerves on edge. Too anxious to eat lunch, she worked through it to get off an hour early.

By the end of the day her neck was whining from trepidation and her shoulders ached from being tense the entire day. She drove straight home and locked herself in her apartment, quickly securing all the windows and drawing the blinds. Still too nervous to eat, she sat on her sofa and simply listened. When her upstairs neighbor slammed a door Chloe nearly came out of her skin.

"This is ridiculous!" She jumped up off the couch and threw her blinds open. "I'm not hiding from him!" Appalled with herself for having raced home to hide away, Chloe snatched up her purse and keys and set out for a rare night alone on the town.

Fifteen minutes later as she pulled her sleek silver Magnum into the parking lot of her favorite Greek restaurant she snorted mockingly. *Dinner alone? Some night on the town.*

Inside the maitre'd led her to a table toward the back of the restaurant.

Still wearing her work attire, she peeled off her ash colored suit coat to reveal a cream sleeveless blouse that perfectly matched the form fitting pencil skirt and heels she'd selected that morning.

The maitre'd took her blazer and her drink order and left her with a menu.

Waiting on her glass of merlot, she reached up and pulled the single pin from her hair that held her waist-length locks in a chignon. When her satiny hair fell in an ebony cascade, she reached up a hand to massage her scalp. It always felt so good to let her hair down. She sighed in appreciation as her fingers worked their glorious magic, her eyes fluttering closed. She was forcing her shoulders to relax when she instantly stilled.

"I had anticipated you dining with us at the compound."

Her eyes snapped open and locked on Dell's as he pulled out the chair opposite her. Chloe pulled her hand from her hair and scooted her chair back. "I was just leaving."

At that moment the maitre'd arrived with her glass of wine. "The lady's wine." He turned to eye Dell, "Something for her gentleman?"

Dell kept his eyes on her, "Draft beer please."

The maitre'd nodded once and disappeared.

Wearing jeans and a form fitting long sleeve thermal shirt, Chloe tried not to notice how every muscle in Dell's chiseled torso was accentuated. While his medium skin tone was a near perfect match to Chloe's, and both had hair black as pitch, the similarities ended there.

Chloe was all business, sitting rod straight. Long bare legs crossed exuding a sensuality that she couldn't disguise if she tried. Her slender fingers fidgeted nervously with her napkin while her almond shaped eyes looked anywhere but at him.

Dell on the other hand was hard as steel. He kept his amber eyes pinned on Chloe, absorbing every gesture and nuance. His large frame was so well-defined that she couldn't help but wonder if he'd kept up with wrestling after high school. His hair was shorn, tapering at his thick neck but long enough on top to have Chloe's fingers itching to run through the satiny-looking strands.

Horrified at actually entertaining such thoughts, she made to stand, but Dell's hand clamped on her forearm had her staying in her seat. The electricity that raced up her arm sent a shiver instantly coursing through her body. She paled dangerously and dropped back into her seat.

Dell quickly removed his hand, "Are you alright?"

Chloe took a few breaths then nodded.

"Take a sip of your wine."

She did as she was told, trying to force the tremble from her limbs as she lifted the glass to her lips. She took a few unsteady sips before replacing her glass and frowning at Dell before demanding, "What did you do to me?"

He sat back in the chair as the maitre'd returned with his drink.

"Are we ready to order?"

"I'm not stayi..."

Dell cut in, "Yes. Two house specials."

The maitre'd shifted his eyes quickly from Chloe to Dell then back. "And would you like to add a soup or salad?"

Dell kept his eyes on Chloe, "Two salads with house dressing."

"Very good, sir." Then the maitre'd turned, grabbed the menus, and left.

"I'm not staying," Chloe argued in a hushed tone.

"You are." Dell put his forearms on the table and leaned in, his nostrils flaring.

"What are you doing," Chloe snapped.

"Smelling you," he responded casually.

She blanched and dropped her eyes to her blouse in uncertainty.

"Relax, you smell fine."

Her eyes lifted to his, "Then why are you..."

"Because it pleases me."

This time they were interrupted by a stout, dark haired, woman who delivered two small plates and a basket of Tsoureki. Having skipped lunch, the scent of the warm braided Greek bread had Chloe's belly growling in demand.

Dell thanked the woman before ripping two sections off the loaf. He placed one on Chloe's plate and lifted the other to his mouth to tear off a healthy portion between perfect white teeth.

Chloe watched him in astonishment. "Good night Mr. Blackbird." She motioned for the maitre'd with every intention of requesting her jacket, but Dell wasn't having it.

"If you get up from this table, I'm going to grab you." He took another bite of bread, "We both know what'll happen if I touch you."

The maitre'd arrived, "Yes ma'am?"

Chloe tore her angry eyes from Dell to stare up at the maitre'd apologetically, "I'm sorry, can…umm…" she turned to eye the table, "can I get more wine please?"

The maitre'd eyed her still full glass then stared at her as if she were an imbecile. "Right away ma'am."

Dell was grinning broadly between bites of his bread as Chloe lifted the wine glass to her lips and quickly drank, trying to make room for her requested re-fill. She was nearly finished when the unmistakable clamor of several sets of heels had her turning.

Three stunning blonde beauties strode in. Each wore a vibrant shade, louder then the next and all wore skirts so short that Chloe wondered if they weren't in some form of thigh flashing competition.

All three appeared to lock eyes on Dell at the same time, and the woman in front stopped dead in her tracks then turned her head to state none to quietly, "Oh my God! I'd have come sooner if I'd have known Adonis was actually going to be here."

The three women erupted into shrill laughter even as Chloe rolled her eyes and turned her attention back to Dell. She was surprised to find him eyeing her and not the trio of sirens that were so obviously interested in him.

When the maitre'd returned, Chloe had succeeded in downing her glass of wine, which had the maitre'd's brows rising. Quietly, he refilled her wine glass then asked if Dell wanted another drink.

Mortification seared her cheeks when Dell responded, "No thanks. One of us has to be able to drive."

Her flush only intensified when the maitre'd responded, "Excellent choice sir."

"Great," she barked in a whisper when the maitre'd left, "now I look like a lush!"

Dell simply shrugged one shoulder carelessly, "You shouldn't worry yourself over how you're perceived."

She bristled as the three women who'd been admiring Dell selected the table directly next to theirs. Chloe pinned Dell with a hard gaze as she crossed her arms over her chest, trying to ignore his admirers at the next table. "Easy for you to say. We don't all have a family compound where we can run and hide from the rest of the world."

A challenging glint lit his eyes, "Is that what you think we're doing? Hiding? Seeking protection from society?"

Chloe simply pursed her lips in response, lifting her brows mockingly in silent confirmation.

"Has it ever occurred to you that perhaps it's for *society's* safety and not our own that we reside in the mountains?"

Uncrossing her arms she eyed the tables around them. Most were vacant, but an elderly coupled occupied a booth in the corner, too far to hear their conversation.

"Is that true?"

Dell shrugged again, finishing the last of the bread. "It's probably best for all parties."

Chloe turned slightly to eye the other table, "Perhaps we shouldn't discuss this here."

Dell kept his eyes on her. "They're too concerned with themselves to bother listening to our conversation."

She chewed on her bottom lip a moment. "Is your family dangerous?"

"Not any more dangerous than yours. But we are different, and people tend to fear that which they don't understand."

"Well can you blame them?" She pulled up her purse and began unzipping it, "You're people apparently posses the power to incapacitate us with a mere touch."

"No, just you."

Chloe stilled. "Why just me?" She watched as Dell's eyes transitioned from a warm amber to nearly black.

"It affects me as well you know?"

"No, I don't know. What affects you?"

"When mates find one another, it is painful for them to touch one another until there is a claiming."

Claiming? She didn't even want to ask. "It doesn't necessarily hurt when you touch me. It's more of a draining really. It's like you take all my energy or something."

"Well it's painful for me."

Chloe dropped her eyes back to her purse, "Then stop doing it!"

Dell laughed then, drawing Chloe's eyes back up to his. His laugh was so genuine, that Chloe too had to smile at her own chastisement.

"You should do that more often."

"What?" she asked, "Admonish you?"

He shook his head slightly, "No, smile."

The curve left her lips then on a sigh as she stated under her breath, "Would I had more reason to."

"I can give you reason to."

She stared at him, and for the briefest moment she actually considered what it would be like to be his; to live at the Blackbird compound, to be a member of his family. Long moments went by with her simply staring at him, and he seemed content to simply let her.

Mom would be so... she'd been about to think how relieved her mother would be if she knew her daughter had finally found a good man, but then she remembered exactly who it was she was dealing with. *Relieved!* She snorted condescendingly. *Mom would die if I betrayed the family in such a manner.*

The dark haired waitress arrived with two plates and Chloe was more than a little relieved to discover that the day's special was lamb steak with Greek potatoes. While she enjoyed Greek food, some of it was too rich for her simple palate.

They ate in silence a few moments before Dell asked around a bite of potato, "Do you come here often?"

She took a sip of wine, "No. I came here on a date last month. I liked it and thought I'd give it a second try."

Dell who'd been chewing quite aggressively stopped. "Date?"

Frowning up at him from dropped lashes, Chloe took a small bit of lamb. "Yes. A date. I do date."

Dell began chewing again, "Anything serious?"

"No, not yet." Chloe watched his throat convulse as he took a healthy drink from his glass of beer.

He set the glass down a little too loudly, "That sounds hideously optimistic."

Her brows hiked, "Hideously optimistic?" She couldn't control the laughter that bubbled forth, "What is that supposed to mean?"

"It just means that you should be cautious. You have no idea what kind of lunatics and psychopaths are running around out there. It's dangerous."

She lifted her elbows to the table and laced her fingers under her chin to eye him accusingly, "Oh, I think I have some idea."

He frowned at her, "I'm serious!"

She dropped her hands and took up her fork before whispering, "So am I."

The remainder of the meal was eaten in silence. Well, relative silence. The cacophony of giggles from the adjoining table only grew louder and more obnoxious with every bottle of wine the trio of bimbos downed.

The waitress returned to check on Chloe and Dell and to remove their plates, then left only to return moments later with the bill. Chloe reached for it, but Dell pulled it from between her fingers.

"You are not paying for my dinner. *This* was not a date." She yanked a crimson wallet out of her matching purse and dropped thirty dollars on the table.

Dell chuckled, placing another thirty on top of hers, "I'll let you pay for yourself, *this* time."

"*This* is the only time there'll ever be. I'm done playing these games with you." Her tirade was interrupted as a chorus of giggles once again broke out from the trio of women at the table beside them. "Look, it's obvious that you can have your choice of women. Take one of them home." She motioned with her chin toward the trio of female admirers.

Dell didn't take his eyes from her. "None of them is my mate."

"Neither am I," she countered.

One corner of his mouth lifted in a wry smile. "That remains to be seen."

Chloe crumpled her napkin and placed it on her plate.

"Fine! What do I have to do to disprove this so-called mating?"

Dell leaned in, watching her intently. "Are you attracted to me Chloe?"

"No!"

He smiled, "I thought I told you that I can smell deceit. And as sweet as yours smells it's disappointing all the same." He tucked the cash into the bill wallet and asked, "Your bags in your car? I'll follow you to the compound."

"Look, there isn't anything that'll be proved by me coming out and staying at your home. Whatever it is you think you need to know you need to find out now." She glanced at her watch, "It's getting late, and I've had a long day at the office."

He straightened in his chair, "I'm afraid that what I need to learn cannot be gleaned in a mere fifteen minute discussion."

Chloe stood, sending the maitre'd rushing for her coat. "Well then, I guess you'll have to live with the disappointment. Good night." Her heels clicked on the earthen tile as she strode toward the door, not even stopping when the maitre'd held out her coat. She simply snatched the article out of his grasp as she passed. In the parking lot she was halfway to her car when footsteps behind her had her looking over her shoulder. Dell was a mere few feet behind her.

"If you try to stop me, I swear I'll scream."

His chuckled response had her quickening her step. "Chloe, I asked you not to force my hand." Luckily for him, she still held her jacket in her hand, leaving her arms exposed. When he reached out and grabbed her by the upper arms she spun quickly.

She'd had every intention of screaming bloody murder, but didn't get the chance. When she turned, her body melted and the last thing she felt was Dell sweeping her feet off the ground before the world dimmed.

Chapter 15

"WHERE IN THE HELL IS MY CAR!"

A loud crash sounded overhead and Briggs smiled at his older brother. "Sounds like your mate is awake."

Dell winced, dropping the pen he held onto the pile of paperwork on his desk as he slowly stood, eyeing the ceiling over their heads. "Any suggestions?"

Briggs grinned broadly, "You could always knock her out again."

Dell frowned darkly at his brother before heading for the door. "Wish me luck."

He took the stairs two at a time until he came to the bedroom door. Inside he could still hear Chloe cursing loudly. Taking a deep breath, he entered the room and ducked just in time as she sent a drinking glass sailing towards his head.

"I swear to God, if you don't let me go, I'll have you arrested for abduction!"

Dell stepped into the room, closing the door behind him. "You're being a little dramatic aren't you?"

"A little..." she scanned the room searching for something else to throw. Finding nothing, she snatched a pillow off the bed and hurled it at him. "Do you think jail time is a little dramatic?"

Dell rolled his eyes bending to pick up a piece of glass.

Chloe crossed her arms over her chest and scowled down at him even as a knock sounded at the door.

"It's open." Dell called still picking up pieces of glass.

A small fair skinned woman with shoulder length brown hair stepped into the room carrying a broom and dust pan. The woman was so small that Chloe first thought it was a child until she took a closer look at her sprite like features.

Wordlessly, the slight woman began sweeping up broken glass as Dell stood motioning toward her. "Chloe this is Stevie. She's mated to my cousin Pony."

As angry as Chloe was, she felt ashamed that another woman was stuck cleaning up her mess. She threw her hands in the air, rolling her eyes, "Oh Christ!" She strode quickly toward Stevie and snatched the broom from her hands. "Give me that!"

Stevie shied back and stared at Chloe, who began sweeping wildly then stopped to frown at the smaller woman. "Oh don't look at me like that. I made the damn mess, I'll clean it up."

She was surprised when Stevie smiled and nodded once before leaving.

Chloe kept sweeping. "She doesn't say much."

Dell bent and held the dustpan at an angle so Chloe could brush the debris into it. "Once she gets to know you, you won't be able to shut her up."

"How long have I been out?" she growled.

"Not long. Took me about fifteen minutes to drive here and you've been asleep another twenty."

When the glass was finally cleared Dell took the broom from Chloe and leaned it against the wall. "Look, I know you don't want to be here. But you can't deny that there's something happening between us." When Chloe opened her mouth to protest, Dell rushed on, "Physically at least." He crossed over to the bed and dropped down on it. "I don't know how it's been for you, but the longer I'm away from you the more painful it gets." He looked at her, "And lately it's been pretty damn excruciating."

Chloe regarded him in leery silence.

"I don't know what's happening to us Chloe, but Mama claims to. The problem is when I'm away from you I can't form a single coherent thought. So for both our sakes, it'd help greatly if you'd agree to stay, just long enough for us to figure out what's happening to us."

She crossed and sat next to him on the bed. "Fine. I'll stay the weekend under two conditions. First, you don't touch me again. Second, when this weekend is over you leave me alone." She didn't expect the grim expression that pulled his features.

"I won't promise to leave you alone Chloe. I can't. But, I will promise to keep from touching you."

She frowned.

"Well, at least until you want me to."

"That," she brushed back a stray strand of hair, "is never going to happen."

Dell simply smiled an odd twinkle in his eyes.

"I need to call my mother. I'll also need to go to my apartment and collect some things."

Dell stood, dusting nothing in particular off his jeans. "You're mother knows you're here and I anticipated your lack of cooperation and had Stevie purchase you some gear last week." He turned and pointed to a dresser, "There are jeans, sweaters, socks..."

"What do you mean my mother knows I'm here?"

"Like I said. I didn't expect your cooperation, so I visited your mother today while you were at work. I told her you and I would be spending the weekend together and..."

Chloe lifted both hands to her temples. "Oh God! I can't believe you told her that. She must think..." she spun on him, anger lighting in her eyes, "You had no right to do that. I don't want her involved in his." She jerked her smart phone from her purse, her heart contracting at the hurt expression on Dell's face as she punched in her mother's number. She had one thought and one thought only. *Damage control!*

"Hello?"

"Hey ma. It's me. Look, I…"

"Chloe, why are you calling? I thought you were going camping for the weekend with Dell. He's such a lovely, handsome fellow. Do you know he called me to ask permission to take you?"

Chloe turned to eye Dell. "Uhh, no ma I didn't. Look I don't want you to think that…"

"Chloe," her mother cut her off. "I know what you're thinking but you're wrong. I want you to be happy. That's all I've ever wanted for any of my children. If that boy makes you happy than you take him, and don't let your own guilt or anyone else's opinion ruin your chance at happiness."

The words were so unexpected that Chloe quickly turned her back to Dell lest he see the tears that sprang forth. She did feel guilty for associating with him. She wanted to hate him as much as she did on the day Donnie had died, but somewhere between then and now she'd given up the fight, and in doing so buried herself in guilt so insurmountable that she hadn't even given thought to what could be if she could just let go of her hatred. She was so confused, so lost, and so scared. She couldn't hide the quiver in her voice, "Mom?"

"Life is too short to be carrying around that heavy burden." The line was silent for a moment as Chloe tried to fight the tears that breached then slid down her cheeks. "Set it down Chloe. Set it down and walk away from it. You're not helping Donnie any by torturing yourself, and you're not proving anything to me. I don't want this dark, angry, hate-filled person that's been traipsing around as a shell of my girl. I want my daughter back, and if Dell Blackbird is the only person on the face of the earth that can bring her back to me, then I thank him for it."

Chloe didn't respond. She couldn't. She was losing the tight grip on the reins of hatred and misery she'd been clutching since Donnie's death. With her mother's words, she felt something break inside and was devastated to realize she'd let her anger and bitterness twist her into something she knew in her heart that she was not. Bitter. She couldn't hate or even blame Dell for what Mace had done. No more than she was at fault for Donnie's actions.

"Baby, I'm gonna go. You have a good time and think about what I said. You only get one shot at life Chloe. Don't waste it. I love you." Then the line went dead.

Still facing the wall, Chloe stood motionless. It was too much to come to terms with now, and she certainly didn't want to do so in front of Dell.

"When you're ready, please come down." Behind her she heard the door open and close as Dell left to allow her to gather herself.

Once he was gone, she crossed numbly to the bed and dropped down, taking up a pillow and burying her face in it. *What have I done? What have I been doing this whole time?*

With her mother's approval, a weight had been lifted. A weight she hadn't even realized she'd been carrying. And with the weight gone, she suddenly realized how tired she'd grown from bearing the burden. She rocked back and forth as a new form of guilt took hold.

I've been behaving like a…a…a petulant child. Oh God, poor Dell. Her thoughts instantly flashed to the day of the funeral when he'd arrived on her doorstep and how rude she'd been. Her poor mother had been appalled. She covered her mouth with her small hand. *Christ, then I asked his mother to leave!*

Now that she'd agreed to stay, she didn't want to. *How can I face them?* She quickly stood and tossed the pillow onto the bed before crossing to the door. In the hall it took her a few moments to find the stairs and even less time to make her way down. She was deposited into a large kitchen, but didn't notice much else as Dell, who'd been sitting on the island counter-top lifted his eyes to her.

"Everything alright?"

Chloe swallowed hard, "Yeah. Look Dell, I don't think that I can sta..."

"Chloe!" The exuberant exclamation had Chloe turning to eye Mama as she came in through the back door carrying two brown paper sacks laden with groceries. "It's so nice to finally have you in our home!"

Mama's eyes twinkled with delight and when Dell crossed to take the burden from her arms she crossed to Chloe to squeeze her tightly in a warm embrace. "Dell said you've eaten dinner, but in the morning I'm making my famous biscuits with chocolate gravy." Mama leaned back and held Chloe at arm's length to stare at her before squeezing her again, "So good to have you."

"Thank you!" Chloe offered in a hushed tone before finding Dell. "Can I, um, talk to you?"

Dell placed the sacks on the counter and bent to kiss his mother's head. "Pony'll bring in the rest." Then he made to grab Chloe's hand, which had her jumping back. "Sorry. I forgot. Come on, we can talk in my office." He led her down a corridor she'd been down before and entered the room at the furthest end. Inside he took a seat at one of the two chairs that sat facing each other in front of the desk. He didn't speak, but simply stared at her waiting for her to initiate the conversation.

"I thought it hurt you to touch me. Seems like a dumb thing to forget!" She was tense and because of it, she instantly reverted to her old habit of insulting him at every opportunity.

Dell just smiled at her wordlessly, his brows hiking in question.

"I'm sorry. That was rude."

His grin broadened. "It *did* hurt to touch you, but for some reason the pain seems to be lessening with every encounter."

Chloe looked at a cushion that sat on the seat opposite him, feigning disinterest. "Will it fade for me too?"

"Why? Dying to get your hands on me?"

She scowled at him, "Don't be an ass."

He laughed and she eyed him then.

He could tell she wanted to speak, but was holding back. "Ask Chloe."

"It doesn't make sense that if we're mates that it would hurt us to touch. Doesn't it make more sense that it's proof that we're *not* meant for each other?" She was startled by the bark of laughter that erupted from him.

Still laughing he stood crossing to hold out a chair, "Have a seat Chloe."

Without a good reason to refuse, she was relegated to accepting the proffered seat. "I-I don't think I should stay."

Dell reclaimed his seat, directly across from her. "This again? I thought the issue was resolved."

"It was but I'm not sure. It's probably not a good idea."

"Why not?"

"I've just had a revelation of sorts and I don't think this is the best place to come to terms with what's happened."

"You don't know any of us Chloe, and we don't know you. There'll be no judgments here. Plus you'll be pampered by Mama's culinary skill and won't have to worry about the monotony of city life or work for the entire weekend." He shrugged a shoulder, "Sounds like the perfect environment to get your head straight."

She knew she'd lose. No matter the excuse, no matter the logic in her argument, she was destined to do Dell's bidding. "Well," she looked around the office, "I'm not just going to be waited on. I'll pull my weight Dell and that's not negotiable."

He smiled approvingly, "I wouldn't expect any less from you Chloe."

"So," she stood, "what do we need to do tonight?"

He reclined in the chair, crossing his hands behind his head. "Depends. Are you hungry?"

She clamped a hand to her belly, "Not in the least. I'm still stuffed from dinner."

"Good, then we have time to play."

"Play?" she eyed him quizzically. "What does that mean?"

He stood and smiled, "Follow me."

Chapter 16

Chloe followed Dell down the hallway to a large sitting room where a fire burned brightly in a large stone hearth. Decorated with dark leather furniture and spaced over an ornate rug, the room felt warm even without the heat loaned from the fireplace. Dell led her to a closet. He pulled out a coat and a matching pair of snowsuit overalls then held them up to her body.

"I'd guess you and Cindy are about the same size." He motioned with his chin to a closed door behind her. "Take these in the bathroom and put them on. I'll go grab you some socks. What size shoe do you wear?"

With her arms full, she used her chin to tuck the clothing down so she could see him, "Six, but…"

He didn't let her finish. He disappeared before she could protest.

Inside the bathroom she frowned at the overalls. She knew Cindy didn't particularly care for her and wondered how angry she'd be once she saw Chloe traipsing around the compound in her clothing. She was contemplating how she was supposed to manage the overalls in her tight skirt when a light knock sounded at the door. When she opened it, Dell shoved more clothing into her arms.

"I got you some long underwear too," his eyes dropped to her bare legs and stayed there, "I don't think you'd be able to...uh..."

"Dell?"

A flush singed his cheekbones as his eyes found hers, "Sorry. I was...what was I saying?"

She grabbed the clothing out of his hand, "I honestly have no idea." She used her hip to close the door then quickly dressed.

When she came out of the bathroom Dell was waiting on her. He too was dressed in cold weather gear, but while she felt like a bulky snowman he was sleek and sexy as hell. Black leather combat boots peeked out from under form fitting jeans. He wore a thick black coat, matching skullcap, and leather gloves.

"Ready?" He smiled eagerly.

"For what? An avalanche?" She slowly shuffled out of the bathroom.

A gloved hand reached for hers and she jerked back.

"It's okay," Dell held up a hand and wiggled the thick fingers. "We've gotta touch skin to skin to be afflicted.

When he reached for her hand a second time she allowed him to close a gloved hand around her slender fingers and draw her down the hall. They crossed through the kitchen where Mama, working some dough on a board, didn't look up as she ordered, "Be careful."

"We will."

Chloe's belly somersaulted. *Why would we need to be careful?*

Outside, Dell led her to the side of the house where two four-wheelers were parked.

"Take your pick." He motioned toward the vehicles.

"Uhh...I...uh."

"They're both basically operated the same so it doesn't matter which one you take." He turned to point at the larger four-wheeler, "Mine's just got a larger motor is all. It's faster, stronger."

Taking a step backward, she frowned apologetically at him, "I'm sorry. I don't know how to drive one of these things."

His eyes grew wide. "You've never driven a four-wheeler?"

"No," she responded sadly. She hadn't experienced much in life. She was always too busy being responsible and playing things safe. Over the course of her young life she'd turned down more offers for exciting adventures than she'd care to ever admit.

He reached out and grabbed her elbow pulling her closer, "It's okay. I'll show you. Climb on." He didn't wait for her to move before he lifted her effortlessly from the ground and placed her on the four-wheeler then began explaining the basics of operation.

After ten minutes he finally quieted and smiled, "So you think you can handle it?"

Chloe winced pulling her gloved fingers from the handlebars and turned to eye his four-wheeler. When she spoke her voice was so low that any other person would have missed it. "Can't I just ride with you?"

As if he hadn't even considered the prospect, Dell sobered momentarily before moving quickly. He jerked the keys out of the ignition and pocketed them before bending and lifting her off the machine to carry her to his.

"You're right," he responded eagerly. These things are pretty difficult to get the hang of. Besides, the terrain'll be rough so it's best you ride instead of drive. I should have suggested it. I apologize."

Smiling to herself, Chloe bit the inside of her cheek to keep from informing him that after his tutorial she was confident that she'd be able to sufficiently operate the machine. The only reason she wanted to ride with him was out of fear that she'd get lost somehow in the unfamiliar area.

She scooted back to give him room to mount the four-wheeler and when he started it and began to pull away, she locked her arms tightly around his waist. She felt vibrations in his back indicating his laughter and, assuming he was laughing at her, she loosened her hold.

Dell drove past the barn and Chloe watched as Briggs and several other males loaded into a black truck similar to Dell's.

"Boys night out?"

Dell slowed to a stop. "They are all unmated males that are viable candidates for your affection. My wolf won't tolerate their proximity to you without having to assert dominance. It's best for everyone if they steer clear of you."

Chloe paled, "Would they…"

Dell smiled, "No. They know better, but I won't tolerate prospective candidates in your presence. It can't be helped. Something in our wolf DNA that forces me to protect you, fight for you."

"Briggs is mated."

Dell shook his head, "No. Briggs is dating. There's a huge difference. While we all like Jessika, she isn't his mate."

"How do you know? Couldn't they learn to love each other?"

"They think they love each other now. But that's not enough. Like I said before, mates are pre-destined. Someone doesn't become your mate simply because you want them to, they either are or aren't."

"What if your selected mate denies you? Would you ever find a replacement?"

Dell heaved a reluctant sigh, "Not that I've heard of."

Chloe smiled snidely, "So I'm your only shot?"

He shrugged once, staring straight ahead. "Looks like it."

Her smile slowly faded, "I'm sorry about that, I wish…"

"I'm not," he cut her off then revved the engine and the four-wheeler pulled away from the compound.

Almost a half mile from the front door of the compound Chloe's eyes snagged on what appeared to be a huge fire pit. Large boulders encircled the pit and it looked as though full trees had been used as the fodder.

"What's that?"

Dell slowed the four-wheeler to a stop. "That's the stronghold." He smiled over his shoulder. "It's where the pack holds ceremony, where we meet."

"Oh."

"Don't worry," he revved the engine, "you'll find out what it's for soon enough."

She wanted to ask what he meant, but bit her tongue instead. They'd never get anywhere if she kept making him stop to answer questions.

They drove for a long time. Chloe had been forced to wrap her arms tightly around his waist when they'd traversed a particularly steep patch of road and when the road leveled out she simply kept her arms where they were.

The scenery was breathtaking. She'd always loved the rugged beauty of Montana and viewing it now with Dell, she knew memories were being created that would imprint themselves on her heart and mind forever.

The early Montana rains gave way to mountain snows that crusted the earth in sparkling crystalline flakes that smelled crisp and fresh, reminding Chloe of Dell's scent. It was strong, masculine, and distinctly Montana.

They traversed higher than she'd ever been on the mountain. The road tapered to a thin strip that crested an extremely narrow pass. Looking down she saw that the ledge was a sheer cliff of around three hundred feet straight down. She buried her face in the back of Dell's coat and felt his body rumble with laughter. A few moments later she pulled her face back to see that they'd successfully navigated the pass.

Finally as the four-wheeler crested a slight hill she saw an adorable cottage nestled under a stand of trees. A dark-skinned couple worked together in front of the cottage, the man chopping wood with an axe while the petite woman stacked the logs against the home.

As Dell and Chloe drew closer, the couple turned and approached.

By the time Dell turned off the four-wheeler's ignition, the couple was stepping through the gate of a worn post and rail fence that encircled the cottage.

"Hi Lloyd!" Dell shouted before embracing the man in a massive hug. He turned and lavished the same on the woman. "So good to see you both."

He turned to Chloe. "Chloe, this is Lloyd Porter and his wife Phyllis."

Chloe extended her hand to accept Lloyds as he beamed at her, "So nice to meet you Chloe." Lloyd looked from her to Dell a bit mischievously, "And how do you all know each other?"

Chloe opened her mouth. "We're...uh..." she turned to eyed Dell, "We're..."

"She's mine." Dell supplied proudly.

Unable to stop the warmth that seeped through her at his claim, Chloe blushed and smiled at Phyllis before shaking her hand.

"Well congratulations!" Lloyd patted Dell on the back, "That's just wonderful. Have you had ceremony?"

Confused Chloe looked at Dell.

"Not yet, but soon."

She made a mental note to ask about this ceremony before Phyllis grabbed her hand and tugged her away, "Let's have some coffee while Lloyd bores your Dell with golf gab."

It was dark by the time they left the Porter's cozy cabin.

Phyllis had done more than supply coffee. They were treated to

the best cinnamon rolls Chloe had ever eaten. The delicious rolls,

steaming coffee and warm conversation created an exceptional

trifecta that had Chloe reluctant to leave. But Dell insisted that if

they didn't leave soon they risked drawing out the pack.

"God loves you and so do we!" Lloyd shouted as Dell and

Chloe drove away.

"Bye! It was nice to meet you." Chloe yelled and waved

over her shoulder until the couple and the cottage were out of

sight.

The four-wheeler whined quietly as they eased their way

back down the mountain road.

She couldn't help but ask, "Are they shifters too?"

"No," Dell smiled over his shoulder, "just long time friends

of the family. Phyllis helped Pony graduate when he was

determined to drop out."

Chloe grinned, "That's nice."

"Yes, they're a rare breed of genuinely kind people."

"They live up there?"

"They come home for the spring and summer. Winters are spent at their home in Oregon."

"What do they consider winter? It's freezing now?"

"They'll leave in a few days. It's why I wanted to introduce you now while I still have the chance."

Chloe wrapped her arms tightly around Dell and rested her cheek against his back as she enjoyed the ride down the mountain and back to the compound.

Chapter 17

Back at the compound, Dell maneuvered the four-wheeler across the property and back to its designated parking spot.

Chloe climbed from the vehicle and Dell followed, removing his gloves before turning to smile at her, "Well, how was it for your first time?"

"Couldn't have been better." She smiled shyly.

Dell watched as Chloe bit her bottom lip, drawing it in between even white teeth as she stared at him. Her lashes lowered and when the wind picked up, Dell was slammed with a familiar scent. He'd scented it the day he'd confronted her in the supermarket parking lot. It had been faint then, barely there, but now it was so strong that his gut clenched. He took in a deep steadying breath and it was a mistake. The scent was drawn deep into him, threatening to buckle his knees and send his wolf surging forth. When he'd first scented it at the supermarket, it had been too subtle for him to pinpoint, but now it was stronger. *Desire!*

He took another deep breath, this time through his mouth in hopes that he'd be able to keep the scent from tempting the wolf that was already close to surfacing. He couldn't deny the overwhelming relief that swamped him when he discovered that she was attracted to him. His balls drew tighter and he was startled to realize that he had hardened, prepared to claim her.

"Are you okay?"

He couldn't miss the alarm in Chloe's tone and realized he'd squared his feet, balled his hands into tight fists and was breathing raggedly as he barely restrained himself from pouncing on her. In that moment he wanted her more than he'd ever wanted anything in his whole life. So much so that he actually feared for her virtue.

He blinked and knew the movement was too slow. Her aroma had him drugged, and like an addict he needed more. He knew better than to breathe in any more of her scent, but he couldn't seem to stop his wolf from surging forth and drawing in a long deep inhalation and even through her bulky winter gear he scented her sweet, heady wetness. His eyes drifted closed and he groaned falling to his knees.

"Dell!" Chloe dropped and grabbed his shoulder and that was all it took.

With animalistic speed he grabbed one wrist and then the other, forcing her to the ground and pinning her with his weight.

Her eyes grew wide in shock. She felt his bare hands clamped on the flesh of her wrists and she waited for the familiar draining to render her unconscious, but it never came. She didn't struggle, already afraid of what she'd done to make Dell so angry.

As he shifted his weight over her, she stilled in understanding as she felt the thick hard length of his erection pressing against her sex. She opened her mouth to speak but didn't get the chance. Dell's mouth dropped to hers and his tongue plunged inside, drawing hers forth and stealing her breath. He held her arms pinned with one of his large hands high over her head while his other hand splayed possessively against her ribcage.

He noted that at first she'd been taken aback, but slowly, she tentatively returned his demanding kiss. And kiss her he did.

His tongue dove deep, savoring the sweet cinnamon taste of her. He wondered if she'd taste just as sweet elsewhere and the thought drew forth a growl so deep and vicious that he'd been certain she would recoil in fear.

When she didn't, he pressed his groin harder against her sex, drawing forth a soft moan from her parted lips that had him dying to claim her. His kiss was brutal, but he couldn't control himself. When he nipped her lip and tasted the coppery tang of blood, he tried to pull back but she followed him. He drew her offended lip between his and sucked her blood into his mouth. He wanted her, *all* of her.

He was lifting his hand higher on her body when his wolf suddenly tensed, sensing something.

Dell pulled back and scanned the area.

"Dell, what's wrong?" Chloe asked breathlessly.

He'd dropped his guard, too consumed with mating to be on alert. It only took him a second to scent the intruder, a shifter not of his pack. He jumped up, pulling Chloe easily up with him in one fluid movement before he shoved her behind him. He scanned the area as his muscles bunched. Whoever had the audacity to interrupt his make-out session was about to pay for it.

There's a stranger on the premises! Cindy's alarmed words carried to him through the pack ties.

"What's happening?" Behind him, Chloe had finally caught her breath and was clearly having trouble understanding the sudden transition in mood.

He was about to answer her when a figure stepped out from the tree line a mere few feet away. The man approached cautiously, hands held high.

"Brother, I come in peace."

Dell growled. There were many ways for an outsider to introduce himself to the Alpha of a territory, and this wasn't one of them.

Dell kept his eyes on the stranger but turned to growl at Chloe, "Get in the house."

She didn't ask any questions, doing as Dell commanded. She rushed from his side and was halfway to the house when the back door was shoved open. Mama stood there, frowning at the stranger, and to Chloe's relief, Cindy suddenly bounded out from the tree line nearest the house, her dark hair pulled back in a tight ponytail. She strode past Chloe, never taking her eyes off the stranger as she eyed him intently.

When Chloe reached the house, Stevie and the girl Hannah brushed past Mama and jogged to take their place next to Cindy and Dell as they confronted the stranger.

"I-is everything alright?"

Like Chloe, Mama kept her eyes fixed on the stranger. "He's a stranger. Uninvited. It's unusual for him to approach in such a manner. It could be considered hostile."

Oh God, the men! Chloe turned to Mama as panic hitched her tone. "Aren't there any mated men in the clan?"

"You betcha!" Pony stepped out of the house followed closely by AJ. The pair casually strode toward Dell and the stranger, seemingly non-pulsed by everyone else's state of alarm.

"Thank God!"

"Mmhmm," Mama nodded her concurrence at the statement.

They watched from a distance unsure of what was happening. After several minutes Chloe asked, "Is AJ mated?"

Mama smiled, "No, but he's too young to be considered a viable mate for you. Dell doesn't consider him a threat."

"A threat? Is that what he thinks of the other men that were sent away? Even Briggs?"

Mama nodded. "It's not Dell. It's his wolf. The males are extremely possessive and protective. None more so than the Alpha. He'd hurt one of them just for looking at you. You belong to him, but he hasn't staked that claim, so right now anyone could claim you. It's a very precarious time. He's more on edge. His instincts are to protect and to claim you."

Chloe blushed and then was relieved when she saw Dell and the pack returning to the house. The stranger followed.

***

"I don't want you going near him!" Dell commanded in clear agitation.

"I-I wouldn't." She was shaking her head even as Dell reached up to help her unzip her bulky coat.

"He'll stay in the barn, we've got a guest house there for these types of situations, but I don't trust him."

"If you don't trust him," Chloe shimmied out of the coat watching him intently, "then why let him stay?"

"I don't have much choice in the matter," he huffed as he hung her coat in the closet and returned to help her unfasten her overalls. "He's from an ally pack, it's proper form for me to welcome him here. Even if..."

Chloe's fingers stilled on the buttons at her hips, "If what?"

"He's a viable mate for you Chloe. For his safety you'll need to stay clear of him. He's been warned that you're here."

Her brows hiked, "Warned that *I'm* here? I'm not a threat. Am I?"

Grabbing her arms, he pulled her until she was inches from his face. His grim features drawn tight, "You are a threat to his well-being because I'd kill him if he approached you."

She smiled weakly intending on teasing him about his suddenly possessive nature, but her smile faded quickly when Dell growled.

"This isn't a game Chloe. When I say I'd kill him I don't mean in the figurative sense." His hold on her arms tightened, "I would literally rip him apart."

She knew the color drained from her face. She tried to regain her composure, but wasn't quick enough.

Dell sighed heavily and dropped his eyes to his hands clamped on her arms before he quickly released her and took a step back. "I'd never hurt you Chloe."

Afraid her voice would reveal her fear she simply nodded.

"Fuck!" he closed his eyes a moment then smiled weakly at her. "Stevie'll take you to your room. Try and get some rest."

"What about you?"

His smile widened, "I'm going to make sure our visitor is secure."

Worried, Chloe fidgeted nervously with her slender fingers before asking, "Would he attack during the night?"

Dell pulled her close and ran large hands over her shoulders then down her back, pressing her body into his. "He wouldn't dare. But as I said, I don't trust him. Cindy and Pony will keep guard over him. Our pack hasn't survived this long by allowing just any wandering wolf into our midst. And you have the least to worry about." His eyes twinkled as she stared at her, "He'd have to get through me to get to you." He bent and kissed the top of her head, "Thanks Stevie."

Turning, Chloe was startled to see the petite Stevie smiling at her from the hallway. Chloe turned to say goodnight to Dell, but he was already gone.

Chapter 18

"How was your ride," Stevie asked as she led Chloe down the hall then up a set of stairs.

"Great. I'd never ridden one before today."

Stevie turned to smile at her, "Did you meet the Porters?"

"Yeah," she nodded, "they seem really nice."

"They are. Phyllis really helped my Pony when he was in his young bad boy days." Stevie stopped at the end of a hall that had doors staggered on either side. One lone door stood at the end of the long hall and was the door that she pushed open. "This is it!"

The first thing Chloe noticed was the masculinity of the room. Probably the size of her apartment, the walls were painted a dark gun smoke gray. To her left a king sized bed was centered against the wall. The bedding was a darker gray than the walls, but the satiny duvet was folded back to reveal crisp white sheets underneath; while a soft looking white fur was folded neatly across the foot of the bed. A tall black leather headboard with an alligator print pattern rose over the bed. Hung neatly above the headboard were two evenly spaced black and gray photos, one of an all white wolf cub and the other of an all black wolf cub. A large charcoal colored rug lay across the floor in the center of the room; as large as it was, it didn't cover nearly half the expanse of the floor.

Shuffling to the black leather bench seat at the foot of the bed, Chloe plopped down and forced her mouth closed. "Wow!"

Stevie laughed, "It is pretty big isn't it?"

"It's," Chloe looked around again, "wow!" She cleared her throat, "But I think you brought me to the wrong room. I was in a different one earlier."

"That's just a guest room," Stevie supplied.

"Then what's this?"

Smiling, Stevie crossed to a door to the right of the bed. "Bathroom's in here." She rapped on the door with a knuckle as she passed it then pointed toward the wall of windows that sat to the left of the bed clear across the room. She stalked to them quickly and opened French doors that Chloe hadn't even realized was there. The long black sheer curtains that fell from the ceiling and covered nearly the entire wall billowed in the cold night breeze. "Balcony's out here, but you won't get much use out of it 'till summer."

Chloe smiled, "I won't be here that long."

Stevie either didn't hear her or ignored the comment as she clicked the doors closed then grabbed something off the small night stand next to the bed before crossing and pressing a remote into Chloe's hands. "This controls the fireplace in case you get cold."

Lifting her head, Chloe was met with a huge hearth that was positioned in the wall at the foot of the bed. It was the largest hearth she'd ever seen, all dark granite that was nearly the length of the wall. Standing, she slowly approached it and realized that the stone mantle was taller than her head. Stepping back she dropped into the lone high back chair that faced the hearth before she lowered her eyes to the remote and hit the button that indicated ignite.

Gasping, she jumped back as a loud whoosh sounded and the entire floor length of the hearth erupted in flames.

The once chilly room instantly warmed and she turned to smile at Stevie.

"I know right!" Stevie smiled back before pointing at a black chest of drawers. "You're clothes are in there." Then without another word Stevie turned and left the room.

Holy shit! Slowly pacing through the room, Chloe tilted her head to read the titles of the books on the night stand before running a hand over the smooth comforter. The room was nicer than any she'd ever stayed in.

After familiarizing herself with the room she took a quick shower and felt out of place when she returned to the room wrapped only in a towel. Quickly, she jerked open one of the drawers Stevie indicated earlier to see what Dell had bought her.

She held up a white glossy whisper of satin that was supposed to be a night gown.

Maybe on my honey moon! She tossed the article back in the drawer and pulled out a plain white t-shirt. She pulled it on and stepped into a fresh pair of panties before taking up a brush to comb out her hair. Loosely braiding it, she flicked off the light and smiled at the still roaring fire place. *Girl could get used to this!*

She was crawling across the bed, her ass in the air and her small t-shirt hiked to the middle of her back when the door opened and Dell entered.

He stilled as Chloe gasped in shock and tore back the covers before rolling to cover her bare legs.

"What are you doing?"

Dell still stood motionless by the door, his eyes slowly darkening.

"Dell!" Chloe barked in annoyance.

He blinked hard then cleared his throat as a slow smile spread across his lips. "Coming to bed. Sorry I caught you unaware. I thought you'd already be sleeping."

"Coming to…" Chloe pulled the covers closer to her chin, "What do you mean coming to bed?"

Dell lifted his arms and yanked his shirt over his head and tossed it on the floor before he bent, unlaced his boots, and toed them off.

As hard as she tried to fight it, she couldn't keep from scanning the bronzed expanse of his smooth, well defined, torso.

Dell's hands went to the button of his jeans, "This is my room and it's bed time. I'm coming to bed."

Chloe quickly dropped her eyes and sat up, poking one satiny leg out from under the covers to let her toes touch the floor. "I'm sorry. I thought I'd be sleeping in here. I didn't..."

When she went to pull her other leg free she heard a beep then the fire went out and the room was instantly black. She shrieked when strong arms caught her in a vice-like grip and pulled her body toward the hard body that was suddenly in bed beside her.

"Don't touch me! What are you doing?" She tensed, waiting for the fainting spell that typically accompanied Dell's touch, but none came.

Dell jerked her lower in the bed, causing her t-shirt to ride up until it was just under her bare breasts. In the dark, she frantically reached up and yanked it back down. "Dell!"

A deep rumble vibrated from his chest as he nuzzled her neck. "Shhh, just sleep."

"I am not sleeping in here with you!" She shoved at his chest before pulling her hands back as if she'd been scalded and he let her go. "What the…" Silence hung between them for a moment as she inched further from his reach. "Why aren't I fainting?"

Dell chuckled in the darkness. "It's fading for you too."

"What's fading?"

In the dark she heard him take in a deep breath as the bed creaked. "From what I've learned, it's painful for mates to touch each other at first. Sometimes, as was the case with us, it is also often painful for the male to even lock eyes with the female. This is to prevent them from dismissing each other. The pain and fainting spells make you aware that there is some reaction to your mate."

"A negative reaction?"

"Negative at first," he amended. "The longer mates are apart without attempting to bond, the more painful it gets. I guess you could say it's nature's way of forcing a mating. After the first initial bouts of discomfort, the reactions will lessen for both the male and female over time and change to bouts of discomfort at being apart."

Chloe wanted to get up off the bed, but was afraid he'd grab for her again, and she wasn't sure if the fainting spells had passed completely. "That doesn't make sense. Why would being hurt by each other attract two people?" She felt the bed shift as Dell sat up.

"Remember the night I first came to your house?"

"Yes."

"If I hadn't been affected by you, I would have said my piece and left and that would have probably been the end of it. But when you triggered something in me, I had no choice but to pursue you to discover what it was that you'd done to me. The longer I trailed you and the more I was exposed to you, the less I was able to resist. I was drawn to you Chloe. Your scent, your beauty, hell even your voice. It's as if you were designed specifically for me. We are a match in every sense, built to be compatible to only each other. Now that I've come to terms with what you are to me, the pain is gone. I can look at you and touch you and not only does it not hurt, it actually feels really good."

She was thankful for the darkness as a blush stole across her cheeks. "What about me? Am I going to stop fainting now every time we touch?"

"I guess it depends," she could hear the amusement in his tone. "Have you accepted what I am to you?"

She didn't answer.

After a few uncomfortable moments of silence the bed shifted again and Dell's voice was closer to her. "Why don't you touch me and find out?"

"No way!" she leaned back and had to catch herself as she nearly tumbled out of bed. "What if it's still the same? I'll pass out again."

"It's bed time Chloe and we're already in bed. What have you got to lose? If anything happens you can just sleep it off."

He was right, and she needed to know. Sure they'd kissed earlier, but she'd been too shocked to faint. Not to mention the fact that the kiss hadn't lasted nearly as long as she'd hoped.

Tentatively she stuck out a hand, not knowing where he was. Her fingers brushed his warm chest and she pulled back quickly.

"Go ahead," he encouraged, "put your hand flat on my chest."

She reached out again and laid her palm gently against the hard wall of his chest and held her breath. She braced for the worst, but after a few moments she realized that nothing was happening. No waves of nausea, no draining sensation. The only feel that remained was the overwhelming sense of being safe and protected.

Timidly she slid her hand over his chest then up onto his shoulder. She lifted her other hand as she got to her knees and faced him. Both hands slid over his warm, smooth muscles. "Nothing's happening."

"Oh, something's happening."

She didn't miss the rumble in his tone. She jerked her hands back. "Sorry." She blushed again, humiliated at how she'd been fondling him.

"Well how'd it feel?"

"Fine."

"Just fine," he challenged. "Did it hurt?"

"No. It felt different. It was," God how did she tell him how good it felt without sounding like an idiot. "nice."

"Nice?" he sounded insulted. "I have told you that I can scent a lie right?"

"That's not a lie, it *did* feel nice."

"You know what I like about you?" Suddenly his hands snaked out and grabbed her hips, yanking her back to the bed until she was pinned under him.

She squealed and tried to kick free, but only managed to lodge her legs on either side of him until he was cradled between her thighs. She stopped pushing at the wall of his chest to pull her too short night shirt down, dismayed that the only thing separating him from her was her thin cotton shirt and an even thinner strip of satin that formed her panties.

"You're lies have a strong sweet scent, like the first lilacs of spring; almost overpowering, but so sweet that you can't help but take in a nose full." He lifted a strong hand to her throat and held her in place as he ran his nose down her forehead, brushed her cheek and buried it in the crook of her neck. "You're half truths on the other hand might be missed by other shifters. They are just a whisper of rose water, almost unnoticeable to anyone who doesn't know your scent." He pulled his nose back and slowly ran his tongue from her collar-bone to the lobe of her ear before he placed a kiss on her throat just behind her ear.

A soft moan eased past her parted lips before her eyes grew large and she clamped her mouth shut. *Oh God!*

Dell growled and the rumbling vibration in his chest had Chloe creaming.

She held her breath, hoping he couldn't scent her desire. When he spoke again, she cringed when he confirmed that he could.

He slid one hand behind her back and clamped her tighter to him, forcing her hips hard into his groin as he growled viciously, "And *that* scent is what I live for." He nipped her ear. "When I first scented it, I didn't know immediately what it was. But when realization dawned, and I knew it was for me and me alone."

He rose over her and while she couldn't see in the dark she knew he was looking directly at her.

"That scent is mine Chloe!"

She shivered at the raw possessiveness of his tone.

"I cannot begin to tell you how hazardous it is for you to even be near an unmated male at this time. Hayden being on this property is extremely dangerous. For everyone's sake, I ask that you stay away from him."

Chloe nodded, forgetting that the room was black. When Dell demanded that she promise she wondered if he had the ability to see in the dark.

"I'll stay away from him."

Dell drew in another slow breath through his nose then moaned. "I know that I cannot claim you now. As much as I want to," he growled, "and God Chloe I fucking want to. I'll give you the time you need to process what is happening." She felt the bed creak again and then Dell's voice was over her somewhere. "I'll sleep in the bathroom. If you need in just get up, I'll hear the movement."

She sat up in the bed, "Won't that be uncomfortable for you?"

She heard him chuckle in the dark. "Not even close to the agony it'd be for me to lie in bed with you and not claim you, especially with you smelling like that."

Chloe dipped her head to sniff at her night shirt.

"Not there Chloe. Lower."

She was grateful for the darkness when her cheeks again flamed in embarrassment. She'd gotten wet for him and he absolutely knew it. She fell back on the bed and tugged the blankets higher hoping to stifle some of the scent.

"Putting a blanket between us won't help. Hell, putting a mile between us wouldn't help."

She didn't know what to say. "I'm sorry. I could sleep elsewhere."

"Don't apologize. Don't ever apologize. And as for sleeping somewhere else, no you can't. I'd follow you no matter where you went. My wolf is eager for me to assert my dominance over you. Don't run from me, it'll call my wolf forth and the hunt will be on."

She shivered at the warning. "Good night then."

"Good night," he growled before she heard the bathroom door click closed.

God what have I gotten myself into?

Chapter 19

The next morning, as promised, Mama had prepared a buffet of hot crumbly biscuits, chocolate gravy, sausages, fruit, and coffee.

Dell filled a mug with steaming coffee before handing a second cup to Chloe. "We'll eat in the office."

Mama winked, "Just as I suspected. There's a table already set up in there for you two."

"Cindy and Pony?" Dell demanded.

"Right here," Cindy spoke from the stairs as she slowly descended. "Pon'll be down in a minute." She eyed the dining room. "Where's our *guest*," she asked mockingly.

"Taking his time coming down I'm sure," Mama pointed her spatula toward the table, "have a seat, I'll make you a plate."

Cindy did as she was told.

"Good morning Grama," AJ entered the kitchen wiping sleep from his eyes. Mama crossed the room with spatula still in hand to grab AJ's shirt, pulling him down so she could kiss the top of his tousled head.

Dell took Chloe's hand and smiled at AJ before he led Chloe down the hall to his office.

"Why aren't we eating with the others?"

"Hayden's not mated," he answered simply.

Chloe knew then that Dell wouldn't be able to handle her in any close proximity to Hayden. Hell, he'd sent his brother away for his own safety. She could only imagine the repercussions to Hayden if he even attempted to push Dell.

Inside the office, Mama had in fact laid out a feast. The desk had been cleared of paperwork and covered with a white linen that housed two plates of steaming biscuits smothered in chocolate gravy next to piles of hickory smoked sausage. The scent was so enticing that Chloe's belly rumbled in impatience.

Dell held out a chair and Chloe took the seat. They ate in silence a few moments when Chloe took a sip of coffee and cleared her throat. "Maybe, with Hayden here and all, it'd be best if I went home today."

Dell stopped chewing momentarily before fingering a sausage and shoving it whole into his mouth. "No."

"Dell, you have to be reasonable. You have a guest, and my presence here is making the situation volatile."

He kept his eyes on his plate, "*Hayden* is making the situation volatile. *You* belong here, he doesn't."

She smiled at his possessive tone. "I could come back next weekend. I would you know."

He took another bite, "You'll stay now."

"You could come to my place." she suggested shyly, keeping her eyes on her plate.

"I can't leave my pack with a stranger amongst them."

She nodded, "Oh." She took a bite of biscuit and it practically melted in her mouth. The saltiness of the flaky bread perfectly complimented the sweet chocolate gravy. "How long will Hayden stay?"

"Not long. It's best for traveling shifters to stay with the Alpha of a territory as a sign of respect. Just settling here without permission could be seen as a challenge. He claims to have personal business to attend and then he'll be gone."

"Do all shifters passing through have to check in?"

Dell laughed, "If they don't want to be viewed as hostile it is best to *check in.*"

"But how would you know if they hadn't? Montana's a large state, someone could travel through one of the other cities and you'd never know."

Dell set his fork down and wiped his mouth with his napkin. "You're right, we wouldn't. But in this city we would. Shifters can sense one another. Not to mention we frequently patrol our territory. We'd know if an unfamiliar shifter were among us."

"How many of you are there?"

"Hundreds in North America. Thousands around the world."

Chloe fidgeted nervously with her napkin.

"Ask." Dell commanded.

Her eyes met his, "How did you come to be this way?"

He sat back and threaded his fingers behind his head. "Our creation story tells of a young woman from our tribe that was kidnapped from her people by an enemy band. She escaped the enemy band only to be caught in a blizzard. A pack of wolves approached and she thought she'd be torn to pieces, but instead they led her to their den where they fed and warmed her. Unable to find her way home and not wanting to go back to the enemy tribe, she remained with the wolves for many years. Over time she came to smell like a wolf and she learned their language. She was a wolf for many years.

One day, an elderly woman was picking berries near the wolves den. The wolves rushed home to warn the young woman who'd now become one of them. She ventured out to spy on the human and discovered that it was her mother. She thanked the wolves and returned to her first family, never forgetting what the wolves had done for her and that they too were her family.

Legend says that when she returned to her mother's camp she took a husband shortly after and when her first child was born it was part human and part wolf." Dell unlaced his fingers, "It is from this woman that we descend."

"Is that true?"

Dell shrugged, "It's what we've been told for generations. Whether it's true or not I don't know. What I do know is that we are born this way."

"Can shifters be created?"

Dell's brows hiked as he smiled, "Do you mean can we change a human into a shifter?"

She nodded.

Sobering Dell shook his head once. "We can, but it in most cases it is forbidden."

"By who?"

"There is a council. It's made up of elder shifters from every continent. For the protection of our kind we've established by-laws for self-governance."

"What would happen if you broke a law?"

"Death." Dell took her plate and stacked it on top of his. "The rules are in place for the safety of us all. We've all agreed to them, so there would be no cause to go against them."

Chloe's eyes grew wide with interest, "Has anyone ever gone against the council and created a shifter?"

Dell pinned her with his amber eyes. "Yes. It's happened before, decades ago. No human has been changed against their will in a very long time."

"Against their will? Are there people that want to be changed?"

A knock sounded at the door and Chloe turned to look at it before returning her eyes to Dell. He stood, scowling at the door. His chin was dropped low to his chest.

Without a response, the door clicked open and Hayden peeked in. "Morning all." He stepped into the room and Dell growled. "Easy big guy. Just wanted to thank you for letting me stay last night." He dropped his eyes to Chloe. "Wow, no wonder he wants you all to himself."

"Get out!"

Chloe turned startled eyes to Dell. His hands were balled into tight fists as he pushed white knuckles into the desk top.

"Hey! What are you doing?"

Chloe recognized Pony's voice from the hall.

"You can't be in there."

Hayden turned to the door and walked out it quickly. Pony peeked his head in and grimaced at Dell. "Sorry bro. Won't happen again."

"Make sure it doesn't," Dell ground out between clenched teeth.

Rubbing her sweaty palms down the front of her jeans, Chloe stood. She knew the tension was the result of Hayden being near her. She felt at fault for the uncomfortable situation, but didn't know a remedy. "Seriously Dell, I'd like to leave and come back once Hayden's gone."

"As I said," Dell frowned at her, "Where you go, I go, but I can't leave the pack unattended with Hayden here."

"So what do we do?"

"We stay."

She cocked her head playfully, "You know a few short days ago you didn't have to go wherever I went. What changed?"

Dell's eyes darkened and he smiled slowly. "You."

"Me?"

He stood and circled the desk before slowly walking to her. When he reached her, he let one hand rest gently on her hip while the other reached up to smooth a thumb along her jaw line. "I don't know how to say this delicately, so I'm just going to say it."

Chloe stared up at him, holding her breath.

"Me bringing you here was supposed to be a trial. I needed to see if there was something between us and see if I could resist that something. I was fully confident that I'd be able to if you chose to walk away, but then last night." His eyes darkened until they were nearly black. "Last night when you..." He smiled, "When I scented your *desire*."

Her cheeks flamed.

"I knew then that I couldn't resist you." He slid his hand down her throat to her shoulder and pulled her harder into him. "My need to be buried deep inside you is almost as consuming as my need to lick every drop of cream from your..."

Chloe gasped, pulling back, but it was too late. She couldn't stop the swell of desire that shot through her and had her moistening in anticipation.

Dell growled and lunged for her, ignoring her shriek as he pulled her close to him and buried his nose in her hair, pressing his body hard into hers. "God Chloe! The more I smell it the stronger the need becomes." He growled deep in his chest, "You're fucking killing me."

He pulled back and eyed her, his face inching closer to hers and she licked her lips in expectantly.

Just then the cell phone in her pocket shrilled. She jumped and frowned at Dell as he pulled back eyeing her pocket.

The phone rang two more times before she finally jerked it free and answered. "Hello?"

"Mornin' sweet cheeks. How'd you sleep?"

Chloe turned her back to Dell, "Fine Marissa, how was your night?"

"Good. I just wanted to call and make sure we're still on for tonight. I called Amanda and Laura and they're totally down for some Blackbird bashing!"

Wincing, Chloe stalked further from Dell hoping he couldn't hear the conversation. "About that," she turned to peek over her shoulder at Dell before lowering her voice, "I'm sorry Mariss, but something's come up."

"Aww, come on! I'm not going to let you mope around your crappy little apartment all weekend."

"I'm not," Chloe answered quickly, "I'm spending the weekend with a friend."

There was silence on the line before Marissa spoke, a smile in her voice. "A *male* friend?"

Chloe didn't want to affirm but knew that her odds of being forgiven for ditching Marissa on a girl's night out would be enhanced by the fact. "Yes."

"Holy shit! Who is it? Anybody I know?"

"No. Look, I'm sorry about tonight Mariss, but I gotta go."

Marissa laughed, "Yes you do. If anybody needs to get proper fucked it's you! Have fun, get laid. Don't over think it."

Feeling her cheeks flame, Chloe rolled her eyes, "Okay, well you guys have a good time tonight."

"Oh, we will, but more importantly *you* have a good time tonight."

Then the line went dead. Slowly turning, Chloe was met with Dell's smile, and knew instantly that he'd heard every word.

"Proper fucked?"

Her cheeks grew hotter, "My friend Marissa, she's a little, uhh, brusque."

Dell crossed his arms over his chest. "Blackbird bashing?"

Mortification seared her and Chloe's mouth fell open. She didn't have a response. "I-We..." She looked down at her phone, "It's a long story."

Nodding once, Dell smiled wider, "Well I'll just take the dishes to the kitchen and when I get back you can start from the beginning." He grabbed the dishes from the desk top and winked at her before he left the room.

"Christ!" Chloe turned her back on the door, lifting her phone to quickly silence the ringer. She checked to make sure she hadn't missed any texts before she turned to smile innocently at Dell as he'd returned.

Her smiled faded when instead of turning to greet Dell, Hayden stood in the doorway.

"Morning beautiful." He casually entered the room.

Chloe eyed the empty doorway. "I-I don't think you should be here."

Hayden flashed a smiled at her, slowly approaching.

Chloe eyed the door again hoping Dell would return. When she looked back to Hayden, he was already beside her, lifting a hand to brush a loose strand of her hair back. "You know Dell's right. You're scent is so intoxicating that any wolf would die to bury his face between your legs."

Shock registered and Chloe instinctively took a step back her mouth dropping wide in offense. When he could have heard any part of her and Dell's conversations, she didn't know.

"Careful love," Hayden crooned advancing on her, "keep those sweet lips parted like that and a man is apt to take it as an invitation to put *something* in there."

Angry now, Chloe clamped her mouth shut and took another step back, but this time her foot caught on something and she tripped. She gasped and reached out in an attempt to catch herself.

Hayden swiftly caught her, hauling her up and wrapping her securely in his strong arms. Chloe shoved at him, but he didn't release her.

"Stop!" Chloe shoved harder, garnering a chuckle from Hayden.

He didn't stop, instead he dipped his head to nuzzle her neck and moan.

"Dell's coming right back," she threatened hoping to scare Hayden off.

"No," he laughed against her throat as his arms snaked about her, turning her more fully into him. "Seems there's a fire out in the barn."

Her heart hammered in her chest. She knew by his nonchalance that Hayden had started the fire. She had to escape.

"STOP!" she shrieked, attempting to lift a knee and drive it into his groin. It was a mistake. He caught her knee and slid his fingers under it, pulling her leg wide to position his hips between her thighs.

She slapped at the hand that slid up her thigh and under her skirt. When she felt the whisper of lace that was her underwear being ripped away fear coursed through her. *He wouldn't.* "STOP! DON'T! DEEEEEEEELLL!"

Hayden ignored her scream, keeping his eyes locked on hers.

When she heard the unmistakable sound of a zipper she began to fight. She slapped at him with one hand and he easily caught it, using her own momentum to turn her until both wrists were captured in his vice-like grip. He took a step and lifted her effortlessly.

When Chloe came down, she was facing the back of the couch. Seconds later Hayden released her hands and put one of his behind her neck forcing her down while the other lifted her skirt. His knee spread her legs and in the flash of two seconds, Chloe was bent over the back of the couch, her bare ass in the air with Hayden behind her.

"STOOOOP!" She screamed as tears sprang forth and she struggled to right herself.

"Once I enter you, he'll no longer want you. You'll belong to me."

She felt him use one foot to kick her legs wider.

"I claim you as *my* mate. Let's hope you last longer than the last one."

Chloe jerked her hips and screamed louder, "STOOOOOOOOP!"

Everything happened so quickly that Chloe barely had a chance to register what was happening. One minute Hayden had her bent over the couch about to enter her, then the next there was a fierce growl and a rush of air swooshing over her, and then she was free.

Quickly righting herself she locked her eyes on the fierce battle that raged in the center of the room. Two large wolves were battling ferociously. The large gray wolf was slightly bigger than the white wolf that tore at the gray wolf's fur. She remembered the gray wolf from the woods and knew it was Dell. The wolves were snarling and snapping as they ripped each other apart.

Chloe jerked her skirt down and scrambled backward until she hit the wall. Vicious snarls rent the air as furniture was shoved back and lamps were sent crashing to the ground. In the distance she could hear the thunder of approaching feet that indicated the pack was coming. She didn't know what to do. Part of her wanted to try and intervene, to stop the melee, but the fighting was so ferocious that she could do nothing but stare wide eyed and wait for the pack to come to the rescue.

Relief rushed her when Cindy entered the room followed closely by Pony. Pony shifted instantly and Cindy reached out just in time to grab the scruff of his neck and haul him back. "No Pony. You can't interfere. They are battling for dominance." Cindy's face paled. "The winner will claim the pack..." She turned to frown at Chloe as she stared back in shock, "and Chloe."

Chloe's hopes that the pack would break up the fight were demolished. Tears flooded her eyes. *Fighting for dominance? Whoever wins will claim me!* She knew that's how it worked in the wild, outsiders had the opportunity to fight the Alpha and claim his pack, his territory, but she'd had no idea it was the same with shifters.

Suddenly the fight carried an all new severity that stifled the room with its weight. Dell could lose, and if he did, he'd lose his pack. But what of her? She wouldn't allow Hayden to claim her.

As the fight drew closer to her, Chloe stood on trembling knees and jumped out of the way. Certain she had a clear shot. She scrambled toward Cindy and Pony but slipped on the broken glass. She hit the floor with a heavy thud and felt a searing pain in her hip that stole her breath. Rolling to her side she saw an expanding stain of crimson blooming on her white gown. Reaching down with trembling fingers, she pulled out a jagged piece of glass that had lodged itself deep in her hip.

Cindy lifted her eyes from Chloe and made it one step as she yelled, "JESUS DELL, DOOOOOOON'T!"

Chloe turned her head just in time to see the large gray wolf she knew to be Dell lock his massive jaws on the throat of the pale wolf. In one fluid movement he lifted, jerked back and rolled, then the white wolf fell limply to the floor and was still.

Cindy had to jump over Chloe's still sprawled form to get to Dell. Chloe watched as Cindy bent and put a hand on the white wolf's throat, when she pulled her hand back it was covered in blood. "Fuck!" Dell stood over the wolf, part of Hayden's throat still clamped between his teeth.

Cindy frowned sadly at Dell as she stood and retrieved a throw blanket from one of the overturned chairs and laid it over the dead wolf. She looked up at Pony, "Get him out of here. Now!"

Pony too jumped over Chloe and helped Cindy wrap the wolf in the blanket before he hoisted the great beast into his arms and disappeared with him down the hall.

Chloe's was struggling to her feet, one hand clamped over the gash in her hip when Dell shifted and advanced on her. She didn't even have time to speak before he grabbed her by the arms and slammed her hard against the wall, pinning her in place with his weight. "What in the hell were you doing?"

"Dell, I didn't...I wasn't..."

"If you think I'll let you play games with me Chloe, you're dead wrong." His eyes were dark with rage, flashing dangerously. His nose touched hers as he snarled inches from her face.

"I'm not playing, I was…" she blanched, aghast at his unwarranted accusation.

"You belong to me Chloe. I won't allow you to mate with another."

Angry now, Chloe lifted her hands and shoved Dell hard. He didn't move, only leaned in closer. "Let me?" Chloe scoffed. "You have absolutely zero say in any choice I make."

A growl tore loose and Dell slammed a fist into the wall next to her head causing Chloe to flinch. When he withdrew his fist, a large gaping hole remained and bits of dusty white dry wall crumpled onto Chloe's shoulder then floor. "I'd see you dead before I'd see you with another."

"You think I'm afraid of dying," Chloe challenged through gritted teeth. "I'd have joined my brother already if it wouldn't leave an irreparable hole in my mother."

Dell's pallor turned ashen and his impossibly black eyes darkened further. "*That* is the only means by which you'll leave me! You need to learn your place."

Seething herself, Chloe didn't wince when for an instant he squeezed her arms too tightly. Instead she glared at him, "Let me go Dell. I belong to no man."

"No, you belong to *this* wolf." He pulled her off the wall, jerking her roughly into him.

"DELL, DON'T!"

Chloe recognized Cindy's voice and was relieved when she felt Dell still. She glared furiously back at him. His crushing grip on her was bruising and had tears flooding her eyes.

"Brother, she's your mate. You don't want to hurt her. You can't claim her like this." Cindy's tone was soothing, calming. "She wasn't being unfaithful. The scent of her desire that still lingers is from wanting you, not him."

Chloe blinked once and her tears fell. She felt Dell's hands relax, his scowl faltered but he continued to growl. She recalled Dell's warning about how an unmated male in any close proximity to her could call forth his wolf. He'd warned that he wouldn't be able to control himself, and Chloe knew now that it was exactly what was happening. She didn't recognize him. His features had darkened, were more severe. He gnashed his teeth together and his dark eyes had her pinned with his angry gaze.

"Look at her Dell." Cindy continued, "You're hurting her. You're hurting your mate."

Chloe felt Dell carefully peel his hands from her. Slowly, Chloe eased off the wall, noting that Dell had stopped growling. She pulled away from him and inched her way toward Cindy.

Cindy held up a hand indicating that Chloe should stop so Chloe froze in mid-step. She watched Cindy for several tense moments as Cindy spoke to her. "He's not himself right now. He's too fresh from the fight. He was aroused when he found you with another viable male. His wolf assumed you were trying to mate another. When he scented your blood..." Cindy tore her eyes from Dell to look at Chloe, "Please don't judge him by this. He cannot control his wolf right now. The need to claim you is driving him insane."

Dell growled and Cindy's eyes slid back to him, "Your enemy is dead. You're mate is safe. She's not going anywhere."

The hell I'm not. The instant it was safe, Chloe had every intention of running from the compound and never returning. She stared at Cindy and watched as the other woman's shoulders visibly relaxed.

"Chloe?"

The regret and pain in Dell's voice was so strong that Chloe nearly turned to look at him. She caught herself before she did. She knew it was finally safe, that Dell had regained control of himself. A sob tore loose as she ran from the room brushing past Cindy. She didn't even return to Dell's room for her things. She dashed out to her car and pulled the keys from where she'd left them tucked in the visor. She raced from the compound without looking back.

Chapter 20

"So how was your weekend with Captain Yummy?" Marissa stood in the doorway to Chloe's office with her legs crossed at the ankle, a cup of steaming coffee in one hand.

Chloe rolled her eyes, "Captain Yummy?" It was Wednesday and she'd successfully avoided Marissa all week long only to be cornered in her own office. She sighed in exasperation, "It was fine."

"It was fine!" Marissa's gray eyes saucered in incredulity. "Come on Chlo. You gotta give me more than that. Please don't be stingy with the details."

Chloe continued to type, her posture stiff. She'd been trying to forget Dell since Sunday and the last thing she needed was her friend hounding her about him, the week had already been long enough. "Look," she stopped typing and turned to face Marissa. "I spent the weekend with Dell Blackbird. Nothing happened."

Marissa uncrossed her ankles, her mouth falling open as she closed the distance to Chloe. "Dell Blackbird?"

"He's Mace's brother. Nothing *is* happening, and nothing is *ever* going to happen between us. It was a polite night out as a form of peacekeeping between our families."

Marissa's shoulders visibly slumped. "Oh." She didn't try to hide the disappointment in her tone. "That's a damn shame, cuz he's the finest piece of ass I've seen in a really long time."

Chloe rolled her eyes again and turned back to her computer.

"Knock, knock. Special delivery."

Chloe turned to the door and the annoying front desk secretary, who stood beaming at Chloe holding a vase full of two dozen yellow roses.

"Somebody's got a special admirer. Yellow, symbolic of a new beginning." The secretary strolled in and placed the vase on Chloe's desk and winked at her, "What have you been starting?" She didn't wait for an answer as she strolled back out of the office.

As much as she didn't want to, Chloe let her eyes find Marissa who stood gaping at her with an ear-to-ear grin.

"Polite night out my ass! You don't get flowers like that for nothing sister."

Chloe opened her mouth to argue, but when Marissa plucked the card from the flowers Chloe jumped to her feet, bumping her hip that had been wounded during Dell's fight with Hayden. She winced but still managed a shrill, "Give me that!"

Marissa waggled the card at her, "If you've got nothing to hide."

Chloe blanched in horror watching as Marissa tore open the small envelope and pulled out the card. *Dear God please don't let him apologize for attacking me!*

Marissa read the card silently, her grin sliding slowly from her face before she peered up at Chloe, "Geez Chlo, what happened?"

Chloe snatched the card and read the two lone words. 'Forgive me.' Tears sprang forth, but she blinked them back. "Nothing," she lied tucking the card back into the flowers and returning to her desk. "He must be apologizing for his family's role in my brother's death."

"It's none of my business," Marissa bent to sniff the flowers, "but it seems to me like he's interested. If he's not a bad guy, you should give him a chance."

Reclaiming her seat and continuing to type with her spine rod straight, Chloe pursed her lips. "Well, for your information he *is* a bad guy, so no, I'm not giving him a chance."

Marissa sighed heavily and shrugged. "What a waste."

***

Dell hoisted the axe high over his head and brought it down, using his arm strength to project it through the log that sat on end. The log split in two and fell away.

"We have enough fire wood." Cindy strolled toward Dell and cracked open a can of soda before handing it to him.

He ignored the offered drink and grabbed another log, standing it on end and lifting the axe.

"Seriously bro, we couldn't burn that much wood in six winters." She was hoping levity would open the door to conversation. When it didn't work she did what always seemed to work for her and got right to the point. "Dell, she'll forgive you she just needs time."

Despite the cool air, his coat was tossed aside and his button up shirt was halfway undone, the sleeves rolled up to reveal corded forearms. "Would you forgive a man that murdered another in front of you then attacked you for nearly being raped?"

Cindy winced. "Well when you put it like that, no."

"There's no other way to put it." Dell continued to chop wood, sweat dripping down his forehead and off the tip of his nose.

"Sure there is." Cindy grabbed an uncut log and set it on end as a make shift seat before sitting on it and taking a sip of her brother's unwanted soda. "We aren't like them Dell. There are rules, protocol. She understands that. You're an Alpha that has yet to assert dominance over his soon to be claimed mate. It made you temporarily irrational. You wouldn't have hurt her."

With one final chop, Dell let the axe stay embedded in the block he used as he straightened and ran a sleeve over his face. "Clearly she doesn't understand that." He jerked the axe free with one hand, "And in case you missed it, I did hurt her."

"Well, you can't just let her go."

"And what do you suggest I do?"

Cindy shrugged negligently, "I dunno. You want me to bring her back?"

He stopped chopping to frown at his sister. "I thought you said she needed time."

Eyeing him over the rim of the can as she took a healthy drink of the soda, she righted it and shook her head. "I just say that type of shit 'cause it's what people expect to hear from a woman, but if I were you I'd hide in her parking lot until she came out then toss her in the trunk and drag her back up here 'till she saw things my way!"

Laughter erupted from Dell and he shook his head, "I have no idea why you're not the Alpha."

Cindy smiled too, "Yeah that makes two of us!"

Chapter 21

By the end of the week Chloe missed Dell terribly, at least she hoped that was the emotion she was feeling. A steady dull ache had settled itself in the center of her chest, and it was reminiscent of the pain she'd suffered over the loss of her brother. Only this was worse. It was self-inflicted and could be cured at any time. But she didn't want to run back to Dell. She was still afraid of what had happened. She'd replayed the scenario a dozen times in her head and she couldn't help but admit her fault in the whole situation. She should have gone after Dell when Hayden entered the room. She never should have allowed him to get close, to touch her.

She knew what Dell had seen when he entered the room, *How humiliating!* He'd warned her of the consequences of being near another male, but she had never believed things could go so far.

She shook her head remembering how he'd slammed her into the wall. He'd been in a jealous rage. Over her. She realized now that he'd been attempting to assert his dominance to make her submit. It was so easy to forget that he was part animal. Wild, virile, uncontrollable.

The most humiliating thing of all wasn't being nearly taken against her will and it wasn't his sister walking in on them and having to talk him down from 'teaching her her place', it was the fact that after all that had happened she still wanted him. It was inexplicable. Hell, it had taken her a full day to even realize that he'd taken a life for her.

Hayden deserved to die. He'd crossed the line that she'd heard Dell warn him of several times, and he'd paid with his life. She shivered at the memory of his rough hands on her. When he told her Dell wouldn't want her once he'd claimed her, she'd been terrified, which was ridiculous because she'd been more afraid of Dell not wanting her than of Hayden actually raping her. *What in the hell is wrong with me?* She knew something had to be for her to be dying to see Dell, to be near him, to touch him after all that had occurred. *No sane woman would ever consider seeing him again.* Perhaps it was the mating bond he spoke of, but she couldn't shake him. She actually feared never seeing him again.

She also feared the consequences and repercussions of Hayden's death.

She wondered if anyone was looking for Hayden, if they'd trace him to the compound, if Dell would be arrested. The thought was terrifying. She could be implicated, she'd been there. She'd noticed that when Hayden died that he had stayed in his wolf form, which was a relief. It'd be much easier to dispose of the body that way.

Dispose of the body? Listen to me, I sound like a psychopath! She reached for her phone and swiped it on, touching the picture icon that would dial her mother.

"Hello?"

"Hey Ma, it's me."

"Chloe, everything alright?"

"Yeah," she lied, "are you free? Do you wanna have dinner?"

There was rustling on the other end of the line. "Well I was just lying down, but sure. Can you give me fifteen to freshen up?"

"Sure. Do you wanna meet at the new steak house by the fairgrounds in thirty-minutes?"

"Okay, see you then."

She had to get out. She needed something to get her mind off Dell. She'd given herself a migraine just thinking about him. Turning to eye the vase of yellow roses on her kitchen table, she ran a hand gingerly over her arm. Over the past few days her skin was starting to become sensitive to anything that touched it. The sensation had started as mere discomfort, but was quickly becoming painful. She remembered Dell had said that it would become physically painful for mates to be apart from each other. She dropped her hand, sickened by the feel of it on her own skin. *God if that's what this is, I'll never be able to stay away.*

***

"Come on son, you'll enjoy it. You need to get out."

Dell frowned at his mother, not wanting to disappoint her but not wanting to accompany the family to dinner either.

"It's the new steak house Dell. How can they fuck that up?" Pony bounded past and dashed to his turquoise colored pickup with AJ quick on his heels.

"Yeah Uncle, how can they fuck that up?" AJ mimicked Pony.

"Hey," Dell growled, "watch your mouth."

AJ halted for a second to eye his uncle, unsure of how much trouble he'd just earned himself. When Dell tore his disapproving eyes from his nephew, AJ climbed into the passenger side seat of Pony's truck and punched Pony in the arm weakly for getting him in trouble.

"Son, come on." Mama waved him to follow as she walked to his truck and climbed in the passenger side seat. Once inside she sat with her hands crossed over her purse on her lap as she waited for Dell to drive her to dinner.

"Shit," he mumbled under his breath as he stalked to his truck.

Twenty minutes later he was seated at the head of a long wooden table in the dimly lit atmosphere of the new steak house.

To his left Mama listened as AJ regaled the table with the story of his and Pony's most recent hunting trip. To Dell's right Cindy mumbled quietly over her two-year old son Isaac's head to speak to her husband Michael. On the opposite end of the table, Stevie and Hannah were arguing about the best way to tie a bib onto Stevie and Pony's daughter Hailey.

Dell pretended to be engrossed in his menu. The pack rarely dined out. The scents and noise were stifling to shifters who could hear every conversation and could smell not only the overpowering aromas coming from the kitchen, but the too heavily applied perfume the women wore and the stench of after shave slapped on men by the handful.

Dell was sifting through the noise, picking up pieces of mundane conversation when it hit him. He dropped the menu he held and lifted his head, drawing the attention of everyone at the table as they quieted to watch him.

Everyone tensed, inhaling deeply and straining to listen. The pack wanted to know what had caused their Alpha to tense so suddenly.

Dell stood and Cindy motioned with her chin, "By the kitchen."

He turned and locked his eyes on Chloe seated in a corner booth, deep in conversation with her mother. She hadn't noticed him yet. He didn't hesitate to close the distance between them, stalking up quietly until his presence next to their table had both women looking up, Bea in delighted surprise and Chloe in utter shock.

***

"Dell Blackbird, so good to see you," Bea crooned.

Chloe stared up at Dell who had his eyes fixed on her. She quickly looked down and picked up her menu. Her heart thundered in her chest.

"Chloe, aren't you going to say hello to Dell?"

Chloe kept her nose poked in the menu. "Hi," she responded coolly.

"Chloe!" her mother chastised.

Chloe lifted her eyes to frown at her disapproving mother before turning to stare reluctantly at Dell, her voice softened with resignation. "Hi."

Dell didn't smile, simply stared.

Bea eyed the restaurant, unsure of where Dell had come from. "Are you dining alone? Would you care to join us?"

Chloe snapped her eyes to her mother and tried to shake her head imperceptibly, but Dell was already accepting the offer.

"I'd love to."

Chloe cringed when he slid into the booth next to her. She shimmied closer to the window to avoid touching him, dismayed that she was now blocked in.

"So," Bea began delighted with their guest, "Chloe tells me she had a wonderful time on your camping trip, too bad you had to pack it in early due to the storm."

Chloe shrunk in her seat.

Pulling his eyes from Chloe, Dell smiled warmly, "If I could go back, things definitely would have been planned differently." He turned to Chloe then, "Things didn't end as I had hoped."

Still eyeing the restaurant, Bea caught sight of the Blackbird clan. "That's your mother isn't it?"

"Yes. Candace." Dell supplied.

Bea began scooting out of the booth, "I've only ever met your mother once. It was quite brief, but she seemed a remarkable woman. I'd like to run over and just say hello. If you two don't mind."

Dell smiled warmly and shook his head.

"Ma!" Chloe's eyes flashed to her mother. "What if the waitress comes? She should be back soon."

Bea eased out of the table and waved a dismissing hand at Chloe before winking. "You know what I like. Order for me."

Then she was alone with Dell. He was so close she could smell him, and God he smelled good. Like smoke and rain, it's what she imagined thunder smelt like…wild.

Chapter 22

"How have you been?"

She kept her eyes on the salt shaker she'd snatched up. Twisting the cap off and back on as it rained white granules onto the table. "Good," she tried to keep her tone light and airy, "You?"

"Fucking miserable!"

The admission had her hands stilling on the salt shaker as she looked up at him.

"I'm sorry for what happened. I hurt you and I don't expect you to forgive me because I can't forgive myself."

She lifted a hand to rub over her arm where she still had bruises. She noted that for the first time in days, her skin didn't crawl at her own touch. "I'm tougher than I look."

He swallowed hard, "I know. You possess more admirable traits than it would initially appear. I'm praying that forgiveness is among them."

She didn't respond.

"At least give me the opportunity to defend myself. I need to explain."

"You didn't give me the opportunity." Her eyes locked on his.

Dell dipped his head, "I know, and I regret it. I attacked you when I should have comforted you."

The waitress arrived at the table, her brows hiked high as she looked from Dell to Chloe. Obviously she'd heard his statement. "Uhh, we ready to order?"

Chloe shot the waitress an annoyed frown, "No, I'm waiting for my mother to return."

The waitress turned to point over her shoulder with her pen. "She already ordered. She said to tell you two to enjoy your dinner; she's eating with his mother." She turned and jabbed her pen in Dell's direction.

Chloe frowned across the room at her mother, who simply waved then returned to her conversation with Mama. *Shit!* She heaved an exasperated sigh. "I'll have the sirloin, medium rare, with a baked potato and steamed carrots."

The waitress jotted then turned to Dell, "For you?"

"Same."

The waitress turned back to Chloe, "Anything to drink?"

Chloe wrapped a small hand around the dark bottle near her silverware. "Another beer."

"For you?" the waitress turned to Dell.

"Just water."

The waitress continued to write as she walked away.

"Look," Chloe's eyes darted up to Dell's then back down, "I really don't want to talk about this. I've been trying to forget about it all week, so if you wouldn't mind."

Dell eyed her for long moments before he reclined back in his seat, his hands falling to his lap. "I'm probably not going to get another chance to explain myself where you're forced to listen. So I apologize, but I'm taking advantage of this opportunity."

The waitress returned and set their drinks on the table then disappeared.

"Chloe, I'm dying here."

The pain in his voice was so raw that Chloe couldn't help but peek up at him. Her heart contracted painfully at the expression on his face.

"Everything was going so well. But when I entered the room and saw you…" He balled his hands into white-knuckled fists and dropped his voice to a whisper, "I don't regret killing him. I only regret doing it so quickly." He took a deep calming breath, his broad chest expanding then relaxing. "I scented you as soon as I stepped back into the house." He looked at her then with sorrowful eyes. "It wasn't sadness or fear, it was overwhelming terror. I knew you were in danger, being hurt, and I was so fucking disgusted with myself for having left you unattended. I should have known." He swiped a hand over his tired features, "When I saw how close he was to claiming you, to taking you from me."

Chloe swallowed hard, emotion thickening her throat at the memory as she blinked back tears.

"I didn't know if he had. Everything happened so fast. When I smelled your blood, I just assumed…" He drew in a ragged breath and frowned at the room before looking back to her. "I thought he'd taken you from me. I thought he'd claimed what was mine and I was so repulsed with myself for having let him beat me to it." He reached out and grabbed her hand, pulling it to his lap and looking down to play with her small fingers. "I couldn't take my rage out on him, he was already dead." He looked up, "That left only you, and I'm sorry. I'm sorry I couldn't control myself. After Donnie's death, I didn't blame Mace, but I blamed what we are. The man should have been able to deny his wolf's claim on an already married woman and I..."

"What?" Chloe's body went rigid, shock coursing through her. She couldn't believe what she was hearing. "Is that what happened? Mace claimed Beverly?" Angry tears flooded her eyes and she gritted in a hushed tone as she sneered at Dell, "Are you fucking kidding me? They all died over this mating shit?" She jerked her hand free and stood, "Let me out!"

Dell didn't move. His shoulders fell when he realized his mistake.

"Let me out, now!" Her tone rose slightly, drawing attention from a few of the nearby tables.

He turned his body slightly. He allowed her to pass then stood and followed her as she stormed out of the restaurant. He was relieved when he glanced over and saw that Cindy had distracted Bea to keep her from noticing her daughter's abrupt departure.

Outside Dell saw Chloe storming across the parking lot. He lifted his nose and scented her anger and her tears. *Fuck!* He jogged to catch up with her and caught her by the elbow. He expected her to turn and slap him but she didn't. It was worse. Instead she turned sad eyes up at him, her lower jaw quivering.

"Is there anything else I need to know that you haven't told me?" Her voice cracked as she fought to retain her composure.

Dell shook his head, his heart breaking at her clear distress. He lifted a hand to her cheek. "I have never intentionally lied to you Chloe. I've only kept things from you that I knew would hurt you."

"And when I find them out anyway?" she challenged. "When I am hurt by them anyway and even more so when I discover that you've intentionally kept me in the dark?"

He didn't respond, just held her gaze.

She jerked her chin from his grasp and turned her back to him, "This is killing me Dell. *All* of this. The deceit, the absurdity of it all, the fact that I want you when I shouldn't."

He grabbed her arm and spun her to face him. "You want me?"

Her eyes thinned to slits, "Don't act as though you didn't know."

"I'd hoped."

"Dell stop, this isn't funny to me."

He grabbed her by both arms and pulled her hard into him, startling her. "This isn't funny to me either." His teeth were clenched so hard that they creaked, "I want you so fucking bad Chloe that I can barely see straight. When I'm near you, when I smell you..." A deep rumble emitted from his chest as he slid his hands under her arms and lifted her, turning them both until she was pinned on the truck behind her. Dell had maneuvered until her legs were wrapped around his hips. He pressed into her, a hand fisted in the hair at the back of her neck forcing her head back as his mouth descended on hers.

She struggled at first, moaning in his mouth and tried to push him away, but as his mouth worked over hers, she lost her fight. She didn't want to fight it anymore, was tired of being the martyr for her family. She felt something with Dell, something she could no longer deny. In his presence was the sole place in the universe where she felt safe and at peace, and right now it was all she wanted, to let that feeling last for as long as he was willing to allow it. She kissed him back and prayed that after tonight she'd finally work him out of her system and be able to fuck and forget Dell Blackbird once and for all.

Her hands gripped his shoulders and she pulled him tighter as her tongue danced with his. She just wanted to feel, to have. To have *him*. She ground her hips against his, growing wet at the pleasure it brought. She'd been so careful around Dell so cautious to keep from making him aware of her desire. Now, she threw caution to the wind. *Let him know!*

Another growl rumbled from Dell's chest and then they were moving. She didn't open her eyes, only hoped that he was taking her some place where they could be alone.

She felt him drop to a knee and opened her eyes, noting he'd carried her into the woods just past the parking lot. She lay back in the soft grass and pulled him with her as he squeezed his hands between them and worked furiously to release the buttons of her blouse. She gripped the hem of his shirt and when she tugged he growled when he had to pull back to jerk the fabric over his head.

He had every intention of falling back on top of her when the sight of her fingering open the button on her jeans had him freezing. His eyes found hers and he was startled by the warm haze of desire that clouded her eyes. When she pushed her jeans down over her the curve of her hips he made the mistake of inhaling. The sharp musk of her desire hit him and he lost all control.

Rough hands grabbed the denim to pull the jeans down her silken legs before he plucked off her shoes, jerked off her jeans, and tossed them aside. His hands gripped her hips, pulling her up onto his lap. She ground against him, and he hardened to forged steel knowing that her scent was marking him. He wanted her, wanted to taste her, to bury himself so deep inside her that part of him would imprint there forever. His engorged cock strained against the fabric of his own jeans dying for release and he reached down and ripped the front of the denim open.

Chloe didn't bother trying to remove her bra, instead she jerked the cups down to expose her breasts. The peaks were stiff with desire and instantly drew Dell's attention. He wrapped an arm around her and eased her back before he fell forward, catching himself with his arms as he dipped his head to suck one nipple into his mouth, forcing an appreciative moan from her soft lips.

He pulled back to stare at her, then his lips found hers with an urgency that she too felt. She didn't want to lose the moment, didn't want someone or something to interfere.

"Take me," she whispered against his mouth.

Dell pulled back and shoved the jeans down his hips. He didn't get the chance to reclaim the position he'd had over her. Instead, she scrambled up and before he could react, Chloe spread her thighs around his hips and impaled herself on his rigid flesh. He stilled himself, not believing the incredible pleasure that swamped him as her tight body fisted around him. When she lifted and eased herself down onto him again, forcing him deeper inside her Dell threw back his head and couldn't contain the growl that rumbled lose from the depths of his soul. *Mine!*

He held Chloe close, her breath fanning his face as she worked herself on him. His hands slid from her lower back, down to cup her rounded ass to assist in her thrusts. He gritted his teeth at the pleasure of her steady pace and the soft moans that left her parted lips. When he could no longer stand it, he eased her back until he was over her.

His hands grasped her creamy thighs and spread them wider to allow him to drive deeper, harder, faster. He pounded into her and when she arched her back, her body tightened with its release as pleasure tore through her. Her nails dug into his thighs and her pussy clenched around his cock. Her vaginal muscles convulsed, sucking at him in hungry demand of his seed. Dell's muscles bunched and he growled as he shot his warm release deep inside his mate.

He fell over her, and then rolled pulling her on top of him. He remained buried inside her and her legs were wrapped around his body as they both fought to stabilize their breathing lying naked and prone on the forest floor.

She moaned quietly and he felt her lips brush against his chest in a feather-light kiss. Then Dell stilled. *FUCK!* He rolled again to pin Chloe to the ground.

Staring up at him, Chloe noticed that he'd grown deathly pale. "Dell! What's wrong?"

He eased from her and quickly jerked his pants up. "Fuck! Fuck! Fuck!"

"What?" Chloe followed his lead and pulled her bra over her breasts then quickly began working the buttons of her blouse with trembling fingers. She eyed the area, but she could see no one. "Is someone coming? Did someone see us?" She let her eyes drift over the area again.

Now fully dressed, Dell retrieved her jeans from where he'd tossed them and handed them to her without looking at her, "Here, put these on."

Chloe grabbed her jeans and quickly shoved in one leg then the other, hoping on one foot as she nearly tipped over. "Dell! What's going on?"

He was searching for her shoes, ignoring her words. When he handed the shoes to her she didn't bend to put them on, simply stood and frowned at him. "What. Is. Going. On?"

"Put your shoes on," he commanded, "we have to go."

"No," she crossed her arms over her chest, a shoe dangling from each hand. "I'm not going anywhere until you tell me what's wrong."

Dell turned his back to her and hissed. When he turned back to her he shoved an angry hand into his short black hair. "We just had unprotected sex!"

Chloe's pursed lips slowly dropped into a horrified frown. She let her arms fall and had to blink back humiliated tears. "I don't have *anything*!"

He grabbed her upper arms, "Of course you don't Chloe. I know that. It's not what I'm saying."

She jerked out of his grip and bent to angrily force her feet into her glittery silver flats before she stood, "Don't worry!" she ground out through clenched teeth. "If I do swell with child I won't chase you down for support." She turned and stomped toward the parking lot.

"Chloe!" the word was a practically snarled.

Ignoring him, she was halfway across the parking lot when he stopped in front of her, bent, and threw her over his shoulder and strode toward his truck.

She wiggled and pushed at his back, "Put me down!"

Now it was his turn to ignore her.

"Dell! Goddamn it put me down!"

"We're going to the compound."

She struggled in his hold, "I can't leave my mother here! Put me down before I scream."

He jerked his passenger side door open and swung her down until she was cradled in his arms before he lifted her to the seat. "Mama will take her home." Then he slammed the door in her face. She reached for the handle, but before she could even jerk on it, he was already climbing in the driver's seat. One large

hand snaked out and fisted in her shirt. "Stay," he ordered.

"I'm not a dog," she slapped at his fist, "and take your

hands off me!"

He ignored her demand as he started the truck, shifted it

into gear and pulled from the restaurant parking lot.

Chapter 23

They rode in silence to the compound. Chloe kept her face toward the window and when Dell scented her tears guilt threatened to eat a hole right through him. "Chloe, I'm sorry if I offended you, it wasn't my intention."

She didn't respond, but he saw her brush at her cheek.

"Chloe?"

"I don't want to talk about it!" Her stuffy nose made her voice sound off.

"Look that was the most amazing experience of my life and I..."

She turned from the window and buried her head in her hands, "Oh God, please shut up! You're just making it worse."

Fuck! He could scent her humiliation and he didn't know how to fix it. Claiming her truly had been the most amazing experience of his life, but saying so now sounded cheesy even to him. *Of course she doesn't believe me!*

He was eyeing the road, nearly home when he saw her clamp a hand to her belly. *Oh shit!* "You alright?"

"Fine!" she bit out sarcastically.

Dell focused searching for Mama through the pack ties until he picked her out and centered on her and the message he wanted to convey. *I need you home now. I've claimed Chloe and I didn't use protection. She's taken my seed. I don't know how I'm going to explain to her what I've just done!*

Mama's voice carried to him telepathically, affirming that she'd gotten his message. *Be home soon.* Then as an aside, *Congratulations son!*

When he pulled the truck to a stop in front of Blackbird compound, Dell exited and strode to the passenger door pulling it wide. Emotions roiled within nearly overwhelming him. His wolf was soaring on a cloud of pure bliss. He'd claimed his mate. She was his now whether she realized it or not. The problem was that he hadn't spoken to her first, hadn't informed her of what would happen, hadn't garnered her acceptance, her approval, her permission.

Chloe didn't move.

"You can come in, or I can carry you in."

She frowned at him before climbing out of the truck and shoving off the hand that he placed passively on her hip. She followed him into the kitchen once he unlocked the door and he turned to look at her. "Something to drink?"

"Beer," she bit out.

He shook his head, "Not tonight, you'll need a clear head."

Chloe rolled her eyes, "Well of course!" She brushed past him as she stomped her way down the hall and into his office. He heard her slam the door behind her and while he was upset that he'd offended her, he was relieved that she was willing to stay and let him have his say.

Twenty minutes later, Cindy flew through the back door. Her eyes were wide and she couldn't hide her grin as she raced forward and clutched the kitchen island dramatically before mouthing, "Oh my God!" Then she whispered, "I can't believe you actually did it!"

Dell groaned and shifted his eyes to the empty doorway. "Where's Mama?"

"Taking Bea home," Cindy waved her hand dismissively at the door. "So tell me what happened," she was practically bubbling with excitement. "When you told her did she just say 'okay' or did you have to coax her into it?"

Dell titled his head back and pain lanced across his features as he breathed in slowly before dropping his head to eye his sister. "I haven't told her."

Cindy's contagious grin faltered, then slowly slipped from place altogether. "You?" She blanched, her tone accusatory, "You haven't told her?"

"It happened too fast. I couldn't control myself," Dell punched the fridge leaving a huge indentation, "Fuck! I didn't *want* to control myself."

Cindy's cheeks puffed when she expelled a pent up breath, "Maybe she'll be okay with it. I mean if she's here, that's something right?" She knew it was bad when Dell dropped to his haunches.

"I threw her over my shoulder and forced her to come." He didn't look up. "She's upset. She thinks I freaked out afterward because I thought she'd given me and STD or because I'd gotten her pregnant."

His sister's eyes saucered, "And you let her believe that?"

"No," he snapped rising to his full height to pace the kitchen, "I told her it was great."

Cindy slapped a hand to her forehead, "Are you a fucking idiot?"

Dell stopped pacing to growl at her.

"I'm humiliated for her and I wasn't even there! Jesus Dell, do you have any idea how shitty that sounds?" She dropped her voice in a mimicking baritone, "Yeah, baby thanks for the sex, it was great."

"I know," Dell rumbled, "but I couldn't tell her the truth."

Cindy's brows shot up, "Well, you're going to have to tell her now!"

He began pacing again and frowned at the door, "Where in the hell is Mama?"

"We can't wait," Cindy eyed the hallway. "You can't leave her in there thinking the worst."

"I'm not telling her without Mama."

"Well we can do some damage control while we wait."

Dell nodded reluctantly and followed his sister down the hall to his office.

***

Inside the office, Chloe sat in one of the leather back chairs and wrapped her arms around her waist. She wished the earth would open up and swallow her. *I'm so fucking stupid!* Tears flooded her eyes and she knew if she held onto them that they'd breach when Dell confronted her and she didn't want to cry in front of him, so alone in his office she wept quietly as she rocked back and forth. She'd betrayed her family and her own sense of honor by practically begging him to fuck her. Now, *he* was insulted by the tryst, and that was more shaming to her than if he'd have simply left her naked in the woods.

She drew in a deep breath trying to control her emotions, even as another pang of humiliation squeezed her belly. She sat straight and dropped a hand to her flat abdomen and rubbed, hoping to alleviate some of the tension that had bundled there on the ride over.

She stood and walked to the window watching as a car pulled up and Cindy bounded out, all smiles. She watched Dell's sister race toward the back door and let her head fall forward to rest on the cool glass. *Well, if he's going to treat me like some common diseased whore who is undeserving of his mighty semen, I'm certainly not going to give him the pleasure of seeing how much it hurts.*

Sawing in a breath of steely resolve she pushed off the window and straightened her clothes before smoothing a hand over her hair. She'd had it pulled back in a tight ponytail but somewhere between fucking Dell in the middle of the forest and being thrown over his shoulder, she'd lost the hair tie and her hair now tumbled loosely around her shoulders.

She straightened her shoulders and wiped at her cheeks when she heard the door click open. She watched as Cindy poked her head in searching the room until her eyes locked on Chloe.

"Hey Chlo," she stepped into the room and when Dell entered on her heels, Chloe steeled herself, pulling on a mask of cool reserve.

"Cindy, nice to see you again. Would you mind giving me a ride home?"

Cindy actually winced and shook her head, "Sorry, we gotta talk first."

"That's right," Chloe lifted her chin, "the great and powerful Blackbird clan. Do as they say or don't do at all right?" She didn't blink when Cindy's expression darkened.

"Watch it Chloe."

"You watch it!" Chloe's brows drew together, "You've been nothing but a bitch to me since the first time we met." Her eyes shifted to pin Dell with an angry gaze, "You must be soooo delighted that he thinks I'm nothing but a common street whore."

"Chloe stop!" Dell bit out angrily.

Cindy shook her head, her expression softening, "He doesn't think that."

"Sure he does," Chloe crossed to sit on the edge of his desk crossing her arms over her chest, "did he tell you how appalled he was at having unprotected sex with me? Like I'm some filthy…" She turned her head feeling her cheeks flame in indignation before she looked back and saw that Cindy was not startled by the revelation. Her eyes shot to Dell as understanding dawned, "So he *did* tell you." She jumped up from the desk, "Nice!" She turned her back on the duo and clamped a hand to her cramping belly.

"It's not like that Chloe," Cindy spoke softly. "He told me it was the most incredible night of his life, but he's not concerned with what you could have given him or any child he could have given you, he's worried about something else."

With her back still turned she heard Dell growl quietly, "Don't."

Cindy continued anyway. "He's a shifter Chloe. The Alpha."

Concentrating on the pain in her abdomen, she nearly missed the words. Her head slowly lifted and she stared at the window as they registered. She spun slowly her eyes huge. *Oh God, how could I have forgotten?* "What does that mean?"

Cindy looked down and Chloe's eyes found Dell, her voice rising, "Dell! What does that mean?"

He opened his mouth but nothing came out as he shook his head. A pained expression on his features. "You asked me once if shifters could create other shifters. I told you it was forbidden in most cases. A mate claiming is the lone exception."

Chloe fought to keep upright as the knots in her belly tightened. The room was suddenly too hot. "Stop fucking around and tell me what's happening."

"When a male shifter claims his mate, she…changes."

"Changes?" She looked to Cindy, but the other woman kept her eyes down.

"My seed begins the process."

"You're what? Your seed?" Chloe's frown faltered as realization dawned. "Your semen?" Her voice rose as her body began to tremble. "What process Dell?" There was genuine fear in her tone, "Is something going to happen to me?" One hand flattened protectively over her belly.

Dell stepped closer and pulled her small hand into his, "It's already begun Chloe. You're changing."

There was a slight tremble in her tone, "Changing how?"

Dell pulled her closer, looping an arm around her waist and dipping his head until his forehead rested on hers. "You're becoming one of us. A shifter."

At first she didn't move as she absorbed the words, then she jerked her hand free and shoved at his chest. "No!" The word escaped her on a shriek of disbelief.

Dell broke his hold and stepped back, allowing her some space.

Chloe was near hysterical, "How do you stop it? Can you stop it?"

He shook his head.

Tears flooded her eyes and she didn't even bother attempting to restrain them, "Did you know?" Her voice was a whisper, "Did you know this would happen to me?"

"Chloe please."

"DID YOU KNOW?" She screamed.

He kept his eyes focused on her. "Yes."

"Oh God!" Chloe turned her back to him, one hand still clamped at her belly while the other covered her mouth as a sob broke loose. She tried to take a step but her knees gave out and before she hit the floor Dell was there. He had her by the arms and eased her to the floor, kneeling beside her as she curled her legs under her to sit on them. One small hand snaked out and clutched at his shirt, "You didn't even ask me." Sobs wracked her slight frame as she lifted hurt eyes to his, "Dell, you didn't even. You just..."

Wrapping her in his arms he kissed the top of her head and held her tightly, "I know baby, I'm sorry. I should have told you. I should have asked."

She simply cried against his chest for long moments, letting the weight of the situation settle onto her. "Will it hurt?"

Dell rubbed her back, "I'm not sure. It hasn't been done within our pack during my lifetime."

She bent her head to her hands and her body wracked with her sobs.

"It's not that bad," Dell continued to rub her back soothingly. "You'll be impervious to illness, the aging rate will slow. You'll be faster and stronger than you ever could have imagined. Your senses will heighten. You'll be better than you were."

When she looked up at him, an angry sneer twisted her features. "Better?" She pulled free and got to her feet as she scowled at him accusatorily, "BETTER?" She turned and stalked to the window. "You did this to me so I'd be better? Be," she spun to scowl at him, "more suitable for *you?*"

"It's not like that Chloe." Dell took a step toward her, but Cindy's hand on his arm prevented him from going to her.

"Has it ever occurred to you," Chloe's head dipped low, "that *you* might not be good enough for *me?*"

Dell turned and walked to the door. "You're angry. You need time. When Mama gets here, " he didn't get to finish.

"I don't need time!" The words were hurled at him in rage. "I could wait a thousand years and still know that you're not half the fucking man I need."

"Chloe, don't!" His words were a warning.

"Don't what? Tell the truth? If I'd have known that I'd be changed against my will, I'd have let Hayden do the fucking job!" When Dell's expression darkened, she knew she'd gone too far, but she didn't care. He had taken her life without asking her, and she had nothing left to fight with.

Dell stalked her, passing by Cindy who reached up and grabbed his arm. He seemed not to notice as he pulled from Cindy's grasp forcing her nails to dig bloody gashes into his flesh. In an instant he had Chloe flattened against the wall, his body pressing into hers as he peered down at her lowered head. His hands, placed against the wall on either side of her held her caged, trapped.

Chloe's eyes grew wide as he dropped one hand to her throat, forcing her face up and her eyes to meet his. She stilled beneath him. Her heart thundered so loudly in her chest, she was certain he'd hear it.

He could scent her pain, her fury, her fear. Her fear angered him. It was his job to protect her, yet here she was terrified of him. Never again, he vowed. This woman, *his* woman would never know fear while in his presence ever again.

"I'm going home," her words were spoken from between clenched teeth.

"No!" The word was more of growl than he intended.

Chloe lifted a hand to peel his fingers from her throat while the other shoved at his chest. "I'm not asking Dell."

He stepped back, allowing her to walk away from him while the wolf inside demanded he drag her to the ground and mount her, force her to submit to her Alpha.

She stalked down the hall and when he made to follow, Cindy's hand on his chest stopped him. "Brother let her go. She's insulted and afraid. She needs time."

"I wasn't trying to insult her," he snapped, his eyes still locked on the empty hallway.

Cindy's lips cocked in a half smile, "Well for not trying, you sure did a good job." She dropped her hand, "She needs to blow off some steam, accept what she's learned. Let her. She'll be back."

Dell gently pushed his sister's hand away. "I can't. She's mine now. I'll not leave her again. Besides," his features darkened in sadness and fear, "the change is already happening. She won't suffer it alone."

Nodding, Cindy smiled weakly, "She'll come 'round. We women are a stubborn lot. We want to be the ones making all the decisions. Have faith in her."

"I do."

Chapter 24

Chloe jerked open the back door with intentions of walking home when Mama's smile met her.

"Good," Mama entered and snagged Chloe's hand in hers, "I'm glad you're still here."

"Mrs. Blackbird," Chloe cleared her throat, swiping the back of one hand over her cheeks in an attempt to hide her tears, "I have to go."

"Not yet," Mama tugged on her hand and led her back to the table. "Sit."

Chloe did as she was ordered and watched as the elderly woman shuffled to the cabinet and pulled out two mugs and a tin of some unknown substance. Mama flipped a knob on the stove that ignited a burner under the kettle that was already resting on the stovetop. She waited for Mama to speak, but the old woman continued to mill about the kitchen setting out small saucers and placing a tea bag in one empty mug while she dolloped the unknown substance into the other. She lifted the mug over her head and Chloe watched as she closed her eyes and mouthed some unheard words.

When the tea kettle whistled, Mama added hot water to the two mugs and returned to the table carrying a tea tray that housed the two mugs, and two saucers with scones.

"Here we go." Mama set the tray down and placed a mug and a plate of scones in front of Chloe.

"Thank you but I'm not hungry. I have to get home."

Mama clucked her tongue, "Tsk, tsk, tsk. You are hungry, and you are hurting." Mama eyed her knowingly, "and I'm not just talking about the pain in your heart." She pointed at the mug. "Drink the tea, it'll help."

Chloe eyed the mug of dark liquid and noticed that Mama had given her the strange concoction and kept the regular tea for herself. Leaning forward she sniffed at it, "What is it?"

"It'll help ease the pain," Mama lifted her mug and sipped at her tea. "Son."

Looking up, Chloe was startled to see Dell slowly enter the room. He stood by the door until Mama motioned for him to take a seat next to Chloe.

"Mrs. Blackbird, I can't stay." She made to rise but Mama's next words stopped her.

"The pain in your stomach will only grow worse." Mama nudged the tea closer to Chloe, "Drink. It's the only thing that'll help."

At that moment the bundle of nerves that had knotted themselves in her belly convulsed painfully. She tried not to wince as she raised a shaky hand and lifted the tea to her lips.

"How much pain will she endure?" Dell asked quietly.

"Some," Mama looked from Dell to Chloe. "You'll need to stay close." Mama looked down and concentrated on folding a cloth napkin on her lap. "You're mere touch will be soothing. *More* will help."

Chloe nearly choked on her tea, but continued to drink it as she noticed the pain receding. In between swallows, she kept the mug at her lips as she watched Mama turn angry eyes on Dell.

"You should have told her what would happen. You should have given her time to accept it. And then you should have asked."

"I know." Dell dipped his head.

Mama turned to Chloe, "What is done cannot be undone. Whether you accept Dell now or refuse him," Dell's head snapped up then, "the change will still occur."

"Can I refuse him?" Chloe felt Dell's eyes shift to her.

"Yes. A claiming does not take away your free will. But you should know that now that he's claimed and mated you, there'll never be another in his life for as long as he lives."

"But Hayden," she heard Dell growl at the mere mention of the name and she rushed on, "Hayden said he wanted to claim me, that he hoped I'd live longer than his first mate."

Shaking her head Mama pursed her lips, "He may have had intercourse with another woman and changed her as he intended to do to you, but neither of you were his true mate. A true mate claiming occurs only once."

"Once for the male?"

"No, once for you both." Mama inhaled slowly and smiled, "You carry his scent now. You always will. No other male, shifter or human, will be able to bear the scent. It'll be subconscious for humans, but they'll reject you. You belong to Dell as he belongs to you. This rare mating is the way our kind ensures our survival. We would never exist if we lived by the marital rules of your society. Our mating has to be for life."

Chloe rubbed her hand gingerly over her belly, noting the pain was almost gone. The information coupled with everything else was too much. She was emotionally and physically exhausted.

"Tonight the changes will occur within you. You'll need Dell, need his strength, his touch to ease the pain. The changes won't be too drastic, nothing you'll visibly notice." Mama turned to Dell, "Son, take her to your room. She needs to eat then rest. It's going to be a long night for her. I'll bring food."

"Am I going to turn into a…" she didn't know how to say it.

"No," Mama smiled and reached out patting her hand.

"Not tonight. *That* change will come with the next full moon.

We'll have ceremony. It'll be beautiful."

Beautiful! Are you fucking kidding? "I'd like to go home."

Mama didn't even look at Chloe as she stood and walked to

the fridge pulling out a package of steaks. "You'll need the pack

during this time Chloe. No one but us will know how to help."

Mama turned then, "Stay at least until it's over, then you can

decide what you'll do."

"Is there somewhere else," she bristled when she felt Dell's

eyes on her, "where I can sleep?"

Poking her head up over the fridge Mama frowned, "You

have every right to be angry with him, but the tea will only help for

part of the night. You'll need your mate for the remainder."

Mama's eyes slid to Dell, "It's only right that he share your pain.

He created it. By dawn, he'll understand probably more fully than

you the sacrifice that your making for the pack."

Anxiety washed over her as she eyed her empty mug.

Fuck! She wished there were more tea.

Ignoring Dell, she slowly stood debating on racing out the back door or going to Dell's room. She was motionless for only a moment before she turned and slowly climbed the stairs to the second floor.

***

In the kitchen, Dell sighed heavily dropping his head into his hands. "I'm sorry Mom. I don't know what happened. I couldn't control myself." He lifted sad eyes, "It wasn't even an option."

Mama pulled a sack of potatoes from the pantry and hoisted them to the countertop. She retrieved a paring knife from the drawer and began peeling potatoes. "You'll need to make sure she eats all of her food. She'll need her strength. She won't want to eat," she lifted her eyes to his, "but persuade her."

"Did you hear what I said?" His tone was harsh, "I'm telling you that I'm out of control and you're talking about food."

Mama didn't stop peeling. "Of course you were out of control. I tell you males often what a mating means." She smiled to herself, "And every one of you ignores my words until it is time for your claiming." She stopped peeling to pin him with her gaze. "We are wolves son. Wolves! We are meant to be wild and free. This," she waved her paring knife around the kitchen, "our ability to be civilized and social with humans. It's a blessing. But make no mistake. When it comes to your mate, no matter how strong you think you are, there will be no controlling your inner wolf."

Dell's shoulders sagged, "But I'm the Alpha, I'm supposed to be stronger."

Jutting out a round hip, Mama braced a bent wrist on it. "Because you're the Alpha, your *wolf* is stronger. I knew there'd be less control for you when you found her."

"So that's it?" he asked sarcastically. "What my wolf wants, my wolf gets because I'm bigger and stronger and I can simply take it?"

Tilting her head from side to side as she averted her eyes and considered his statement Mama pursed her lips before simply replying, "Yes."

"Christ," he shoved up from the table. "I'm going up."

"Son!"

He stopped but didn't turn around.

"Have you ever seen a dry creek bed?"

Confusion knitted his brow as he turned to frown at his mother.

"When the snows melt and a sliver of water finally slices through only to be sopped up by the parched earth?"

Dell shook his head.

"The creek bed needs to be filled with water to become a mighty river, to become what it is meant to be. You'll have to help your mate change tonight." Mama dropped her eyes to her potatoes and began cubing them. "Fill her to help her become what she is meant to be."

"She hates me right now, and *that* is the last thing she'll be receptive to."

Mama smiled, "Her body will yearn for yours. It's part of the change. Trust in it."

Chapter 25

Sitting alone in front of the roaring fireplace, Chloe didn't move. Shocked by the events of the day, all she could do was simply stare and replay what had happened.

She woke up that morning missing Dell more than she'd ever missed anyone in her life. Then as if conjured up by her thoughts he'd appeared at her dinner table just as she'd decided to finally forget about him. Her cheeks singed at the memory of making love to him in the tall grass and she slowly shook her head. What had gotten into her? It was so out of character, but she couldn't control herself. She'd wanted him, needed him.

Now, a mere few hours later she sat once again a prisoner in his home and now changed forever.

A wolf! Really? She tried to imagine herself shifting to wolf form, but the image only made her nauseated. *Or is it the change?* Mama had told her the tea would work temporarily against the pain, and she was terrified to discover just how bad it would get.

Rubbing a hand gingerly over her belly she looked down when warm tears dropped onto her hand. She was afraid, and she wanted Dell. She swiped angrily at her tears refusing to go to him. *This is his fault!* Her lower lip trembled, *Mama said he was supposed to ask me before changing me, but he didn't!* And that meant that he either didn't care for her opinion on the matter or didn't care at all. She wanted a choice, but it was too late. It was done and she couldn't bring herself to accept what had happened.

She thought of her mother and doubled over in the chair, her arms wrapping around her mid-section. *Oh Ma!* Would her mother accept her for what she'd done, what she would become?

The door opened and Chloe turned to frown with tear-filled eyes at Dell.

"Mama will bring food when it's ready," his words were quiet.

Ignoring him she turned her heated gaze back to the fire and slowly rocked her upper body back and forth. She refused to look at him when he approached and stood next to her.

"You can hate me Chloe. You have the right to, but tonight," He bent and picked her up.

She shoved at his chest and struggled in his arms, but he wouldn't release her.

"Tonight you need me to be strong for you, to be here for you." He stalked to the bed, "And that's exactly what I'm going to do." He set her down and the bed sunk with his weight when he settled onto the bed next to her.

She tried to crawl away from him, but a large arm snaked around her waist and pulled her back into the solid wall of his chest.

Keeping his arm firmly around her, Dell lay behind her and pulled her into the warm cradle of his body.

Chloe tensed knowing she should get away from him, but she was terrified.

"Relax love."

Her teeth gnashed, "Love?" She turned to scowl at him over a slender shoulder. "So I'm your love now?"

Dell's brows drew together and he grabbed her jaw gently, keeping her from turning away. "You've always been my love Chloe. I just didn't know it until now."

She jerked her chin free of his grasp, "I don't want your pity Dell. Or your guilt."

He rolled her onto her back and pinned her body under his. Stormy amber eyes darkened dangerously. "I offer you neither." He let his eyes rove her features before his expression softened. He lifted a thumb to swipe away one of her tears. "I give you my love Chloe." His eyes searched hers, "And whether you want it or not, it is yours. *All* my love, all my heart." He dropped his head and gently kissed her lips.

Chloe sucked in a breath when his lips brushed hers. "Don't." She turned her head and stilled when he growled.

"Look at me Chloe."

She didn't move.

"Look at me!" Dell commanded angrily drawing her eyes back to his. "There's nothing I can do about the change that's going to happen, about what you'll become. But if you don't want *me* Chloe, if you don't want us." His words stalled as he drew in a shaky breath and dropped his eyes to her lips. "I'll accept your decision. I won't like it and I'll try not to fight against it, to let you go, but for you," his eyes found hers, "I'll do it."

Trembling under his weight, Chloe was shocked to see the emotion that glistened in his eyes. "You'll let me go. Let me live my life in peace?"

He dropped his eyes to her throat, "If that is what you want."

"And if I found another?"

His eyes snapped to hers and Chloe gasped at the rage in them. "There will be no other. Not now. Not ever Chloe. You may leave here and choose to be away from me, but you will always be mine!" His face inched closer to hers, "Don't ever forget that!"

Chloe stared at his angry eyes before finally turning her head to stare out the window. "I-I don't know what I want Dell. I might have chosen this," she looked at him, "chosen you." She swallowed hard, "But I wasn't given a choice. I don't know what's going to happen. I'm scared and I'm worried for my mother. I need to know what all of this means. What's going to happen to me?"

Sighing, Dell rolled her to her side and pulled her back until he was spooning her. "It'll be alright Chloe, I swear it. Once the change takes place tonight, you'll shift on the first full moon."

"The ceremony?" she asked tremulously.

Dell stalled for a moment. "The ceremony Mama was referring to is a wedding ceremony. Typically when a female is changed it is out of mutual affection. Her wedding night marks her first steps into our world."

Hugging her arms tighter to her body Chloe winced when the pain she'd suffered earlier slowly began to ebb its way back into her midsection. "So what about us?"

He breathed heavily into her hair. "You'll still change, regardless. It'll be a different type of ceremony, a welcoming."

"And then?"

"Then you'll be one of us. A member of our pack. You're expected to reside here at the compound, but because of our circumstances I can permit you to reside offsite."

"Permit me?" she couldn't disguise the sarcasm in her voice.

"I am the Alpha Chloe. You must comply with my commands."

"Or what," she bit out angrily, "you'll kick me out of your pack?"

"No," he rolled her again until she was staring up at him. "I won't need to. As Alpha I can compel any member of my pack to do as I command."

Delicate brows furrowed, "Compel?"

"Forget it," he fell back against the bed and stared up at the ceiling.

"No," Chloe rolled until she was hovering over him, "what do you mean *compel*?"

His eyes darted to hers then back to the ceiling. "Induce."

Her eyes widened, "You mean force?"

"Not the way your thinking." He looked at her, "I'd never hurt you Chloe."

"Then force how?"

"I'm the pack leader Chloe. All members are required to obey."

She made to get up, but his hand on her arm stopped her. "Let me get this straight. I'm going to be a member to a pack where the Alpha can force me to do things that I don't necessarily want to do?" She twisted her arm, "Could you compel me to have sex with you?" When he didn't answer she prodded, "Dell?"

"I would never do that."

"But you could?" she demanded angrily.

"It *could* be done," he got up and turned to tower over her as she sat perched on the edge of the bed, "but I'd never do that to you Chloe."

"Dell what do you expect me to…" her words died and she paled dangerously. Her hands clamped on her belly and she held her breath.

"CHLOE!" Dropping to his knees in front of her Dell grabbed her hands, "You've got to breathe through it baby."

She shook her head and her hands clawed tighter into her belly.

"Breathe Chloe damn it!"

She sawed in a ragged breath and it was expelled just as quickly on a long moan. Her fingers found his shoulder and clawed in the material of his shirt. "Deeeeeeell?"

Dell quickly got to his feet and lifted her from the bed. He sat and cradled her on his lap while one hand rubbed fervently at her back. "It's gonna be okay." His eyes lifted and relief swamped him when Mama entered carrying a tray of food. The look of confusion on her face was disturbing.

Mama set the tray down on the dresser. "She shouldn't be this bad this soon." She approached and lifted a hand to Chloe's cheek. "Hmmm."

"What?" Dell barked. He stood with Chloe still in his arms to pace the room as he gently rocked her while she continued to moan. "What does that mean? What's happening?"

Mama shrugged, "You're the Alpha. Things are always different with the Alpha. Stronger, more powerful."

Dell cursed under his breath and looked at Chloe. Her face was no longer ashen, but now highly flushed. Sweat beaded on her forehead and her hands, still clamped at her belly, began to tremble. "What do I do?"

"What I told you do to," Mama crossed to the door and pulled it open, "help her change, or watch her suffer through it." She exited the room quietly, pulling the door firmly closed behind her.

Chapter 26

Dell's eyes dropped to Chloe's flushed features that were contorted in pain. He wanted her, he always wanted her, but how did he convince her that sex would ease her pain. It sounded ridiculous and advantageous even to him.

He turned sad eyes to the untouched tray of food. He knew she'd need the strength the nourishment would provide, but now there was no hope of getting her to eat. "Chloe, can you eat?"

She just moaned and lifted a trembling fist to ball it in the front of his shirt as she turned her head and panted against his chest.

Fuck! He crossed to the bed and tried to set her down, but her fist tightened in his shirt.

"No."

"It's okay baby," he crooned, "I'm right here. I'm not going anywhere."

Chloe released her hand and Dell placed her on the bed. She instantly curled into a tight ball, pulling her knees close to her chest.

Dell ripped off his shirt while toeing off his shoes. He quickly stripped then started removing Chloe's shoes. When he'd gotten her socks and shoes off, he used strong hands to rip the back of her shirt and began peeling it from her clammy skin.

"What are you doing?"

"Making you comfortable," he lied.

Her hand clamped over her shirt at her breast to hold it in place. "I'm cold."

"You're burning up love." He tugged on her shirt, "Trust me Chloe."

She loosened her grip and allowed him to remove her shirt. He threw the tattered garment on the floor then rolled her to unfasten her jeans and pulled them from her legs.

The fire still burned brightly in the hearth, so Dell crossed and flicked off the light casting the room into a warm glow. He peeled back the covers on the bed and lifted Chloe to place her between the sheets before he climbed in beside her and pulled her into his arms.

Her slight form shivered and she cuddled closer to his warmth before she froze. "Are you naked?"

He winced. "Yes."

Her confused eyes found his, "Why?"

He had to tell her. "Chloe, the transition is going to be difficult. I can lessen your pain, if you let me."

"What?"

"I spoke with Mama. She said you're body needs…" he tightened his hold on her. "My DNA will quicken the transition. The more of me you have, the easier it'll be on you."

She tilted her head to frown up at him. Sweat beaded on her nose and forehead. "DNA?"

His mouth lifted at one corner, but his eyes remained serious. "We need to make love Chloe. I need to claim you, mate you."

She shivered and dropped her head back to where it rested on his arm. "Is there another way?"

He couldn't help the stab of rejection that pierced him. "No."

"Can we wait? See if I can tough it out?"

"We can." He pulled her closer and kissed the top of her head, "But know that if it gets too bad, I won't ask your permission Chloe. I'm not going to let you suffer when I can ease your pain."

She merely nodded and drew in a deep breath. There was silence between them before she spoke. "I'm sorry Dell."

"For what?"

"For this. For what you'll have to do if I'm not strong enough. I don't want you to have to take me that way, out of obligation."

"It isn't obligation Chloe, and I'm looking forward to easing your pain." He quieted for only a moment. "And I'm the one who's sorry Chloe. I should have prepared you. I should have *asked* you." While part of him felt guilt over his actions, the wolf within didn't bother disguising his pure joy. She was going to change tonight! She was so close to being his that he could taste it. *His* mate. His!

***

Chloe had dozed off from the exhaustion of fighting the change. She'd struggled for hours, relegated to simply focusing on breathing to get through the worst of it. Finally, her worn muscles had relaxed when sleep had claimed her.

Pain tore through her abdomen and forced her awake as she sat bolt upright and gasped in agony.

"Chloe!" Dell sat up and grabbed her arms.

Throwing the blankets off, she scrambled to the edge of the bed. She dropped her feet to the floor and made to stand but her knees buckled and she fell to the floor as tears streamed down her cheeks. Her belly spasmed painfully and she moaned in anguish. She bit her bottom lip to suppress a scream and wasn't surprised when she tasted the coppery tang of her own blood.

Dell knelt on the floor beside her. "It's happening." He brushed the hair back from her face. "Are you okay, can you handle it?"

Unable to speak she shook her head before sawing in a ragged breath. "Dell…" there was a quiver in her voice.

Her plea was all he needed. Dell lifted her body easily until she was positioned on her knees with her upper body bent over the bed. His strong hands ripped away the whisper of lace that was her panties and he slid a finger to her entrance. He was relieved to find her wet. Her body was in fact ready to take him. He nudged her legs wider and rose on his own knees behind her nudging the head of his cock against her pussy. He was startled when she didn't wait for him, but thrust back and took him to the hilt on one loud moan.

"Please Dell," she panted, "make it stop!"

He grabbed her hips and began thrusting into her. His hips slammed into her ass for several moments before he quickened his thrusts wanting to fill her quickly to ease her pain. She screamed his name and he felt her tighten around him with her climax. The fist like grip around him had his warm seed jetting deep inside her.

When his release shot into her, Chloe felt warmth blossom in her abdomen and lance through her limbs. The pain ebbed but didn't disappear entirely. She lay flat on the bed with Dell still buried deep inside her as her shaking muscles whined. She turned her head and her imploring eyes met his as he rested over her back.

"Again?" His eyes were serious.

Chloe's eyes dipped to his bare thigh that braced her own. "Can you?"

He smiled challengingly, "I'm only part man Chloe." He slowly pulled his still rigid cock nearly out of her before driving it deep. "Remember that."

He fucked her repeatedly until her body was finally sated and her eyes drifted closed as the exhaustion and relief from the pain finally overwhelmed her. Sleep claimed her while Dell was still buried deep inside her.

Easing from her Dell lifted her from the floor and placed her under the covers before disappearing into the bathroom to return with a warm, wet, cloth. He gently swiped her brow and her cheeks before pulling back the covers to clean the evidence of their love making from between her thighs. Then he climbed into bed behind her and pulled her into his arms, praying that the change would finally occur and grant his mate the rest she so desperately

needed.

Chapter 27

Chloe woke and tried to stretch but the soreness that tore through her limbs had her eyes snapping open. Memory came flooding back and she lifted her hands to cover her face as mortification seared her. She'd begged Dell to make love to her and he had. Repeatedly!

God what have I done! If it wasn't for the change... She didn't finish the thought, knowing it wasn't true before she'd even thought it. She'd wanted Dell. From the first moment she'd laid eyes on him in high school until the moment he strode back into her life at Donnie's funeral. She wouldn't bother lying to herself any longer.

Dropping her hands and slowly tilting her head, she was relieved to discover that she was alone in the bed. Moving her legs, she winced at the stiffness in her muscles. Her whole body felt battered. She lifted the blanket and saw that she was still completely naked.

Glancing around the room she noted that the fire was out, but faint light filtered through the wood slats of the blinds. She shifted her eyes to the ceiling and assessed her body. She didn't

feel any different. She wiggled her fingers and her toes.

Everything seems to be working normally. She took a deep breath

and her belly rumbled loudly at the scent of French toast, bacon,

eggs, and coffee wafting through the room.

Propping herself on an elbow she scanned the room

searching for the tray of food, but there was none. *Funny, I can*

smell...

Just then the door opened and Dell strode in. He was

dressed in his typical jeans, work boots, and form fitting

undershirt. His eyes met hers and he entered and crossed the room

to her carrying a tray of food. "Morning beautiful."

Chloe lifted a self-conscious hand to her hair and tried to

smooth it down. "Morning," she whispered weakly.

"You've gotta be starving." He placed the tray on her lap

when she reclined back against the head board. "You need to eat it

all."

She looked down at the plate and nearly moaned in

appreciation at the pile of syrupy French toast, three steaming eggs, and heap of crisp bacon slices. Her hand instantly reached for the mug of already creamed coffee. "I'm starving!"

She sipped at the coffee before replacing the mug on the tray and taking up the fork to attack the plate. She was on her fifth bite when a noise caught her attention and she stopped chewing. She looked up at Dell quizzically as he watched her eat.

"Mama dropped something in the kitchen," he supplied calmly.

"Oh," she spoke around her bite of French toast and lifted another bite to her lips before she stopped. Her shocked eyes found Dell's as she swallowed down the food in her mouth. "How did I hear that?"

His lips curved in a smile, "One of the shifter perks." He pointed to her plate, "You're sense of smell should be greatly improved as well."

Chloe eyed her plate and remembered that she'd known exactly what Mama had cooked for breakfast before Dell had even brought the plate into the room.

She inhaled deeply, but could only smell the food on the plate in front of her. Her eyes lifted to focus on the wall as she strained to listen.

She heard Cindy's voice from somewhere in the house. "Do you think she'll forgive him?"

"I'm sure her heart already has, she just needs to talk her mind into accepting it." Mama's response was crystal clear.

"I hear Mama and Cindy!" she lifted startled eyes to Dell. "Where are they?"

"Still in the kitchen," Dell crossed his arms over his chest as he smiled at her. "It'll take you a while to filter out the stuff you don't want, but once you get the hang of it it's pretty useful."

A noise outside drew her attention and she tried shifting the tray of food off her lap to inspect, but Dell's large hand on her shoulder prevented her from getting up. "Eat," he ordered. "You can get accustomed to your new senses after you've finished your meal and rested."

"Fine," she pouted pulling the tray fully back onto her lap and reclaiming the fork.

Dell watched her a few more moments before he disappeared into the bathroom. She heard him turn on the bath before he came back into the room. He didn't approach her instead he crossed to stare out the window while he waited for her to finish her breakfast.

Chloe ate as much as she could and when she couldn't take another bite she inched out of the bed, careful to pull a sheet with her to cover her bare body.

"Ready?" Dell ripped off his shirt as he crossed to her.

Her eyes darted from his bare chest to the bathroom, "For what?"

"For our bath?"

"Uhh, *our?*"

He rolled his eyes as his fingers quickly unsnapped his jeans as he kicked out of his shoes before his thumbs shoved the denim down over his lean hips. "You're still weak Chloe."

"I think I can bathe myself."

"No." He was completely naked as he strode toward her angrily. One hand reached up and pulled the sheet from where she had it clamped just above her chest.

"Dell!" she gasped reaching for the sheet.

He smiled and dropped it to the ground before scooping her up to cradle her in his arms as she attempted unsuccessfully to cover her intimate parts.

"Umm, about last night," she wanted to get an explanation out before anything else happened between them.

Dell carried her to the bathroom, "Don't!" he growled.

"But you don't even know what I was going to say," she avoided looking at him.

He stepped into the large Jacuzzi tub and lowered himself and Chloe into the steaming water. Her flesh instantly bristled in goose bumps. It took her a moment to get used to the water, and when she did it was bliss.

Dell kept her settled on his lap. "You're going to attempt to denounce what happened between us. You're going to say it was the change or Mama's tea, or any other excuse you can think of to push me away." He cupped one large hand and lifted it to pour hot water down Chloe's back. "Look at me."

She arched her back at the hot water pouring down it and followed his command in time to see his eyes dip to her breasts as they thrust forward with her body's arch. Instantly she hunched over trying to fold in on herself to keep him from getting the wrong idea.

Smiling Dell commanded again, "Look at me Chloe." When she did he continued, "What happened between us last night was meant to happen. You belong to me. You were destined to be mine."

She opened her mouth to argue but Dell's wet fingers on her lips silenced her. His amber eyes found hers. "If there had been any thought of ever letting you go, it's dead now. After last night," he drew in a deep breath and grabbed her chin to keep her from looking away. "I'll never let you go Chloe. I refuse to live without you."

She blinked back tears at the emotion in his eyes and when she finally opened her mouth to speak, he simply covered it with his own.

After long moments he pulled back. "I want you to say you'll willingly be my mate Chloe. I want you to accept what we are to each other." His hand slid up her jaw to cup the side of her face, "I want you to say that you'll marry me."

She gaped at him before clamping her mouth shut and climbing off his lap.

He let her go, but when she lifted a foot to climb out of the tub his hands snaked out so quickly she nearly fell when he jerked her back down. His hands were strong though, and he knew exactly what he was doing.

There was a loud splash and Chloe shrieked before she swiped the water from her face and realized he'd settled her back on his lap except this time she was straddling his hips, the hard length of his erection pressing against her bare pussy.

She sputtered from the water on her face and when she opened her eyes it was only long enough to see that Dell's eyes had transitioned to all black. She was learning quickly that the change meant he was fighting to keep his wolf leashed.

His mouth crashed down on hers. All the gentleness of the first kiss was gone. This kiss was urgent, passionate, demanding. The taste was so irresistible that Chloe couldn't help but return the fervor.

Her arms wound around his neck even as she silently cursed her lack of will power. When her pebbled nipples brushed against his bare chest, she pulled back to suck in a shaky breath. Her hips rocked against the thick length of his shaft and her sex flared to life demanding satisfaction.

Her mouth found his even as his hands slid down her wet back to cup her bare ass, lifting her higher as he spread her cheeks and forced her closer to grind against her clit.

She tried to scoot even tighter on his lap but he released her ass and lowered a hand to her abdomen to keep her from sinking onto his cock.

"Please," she begged breathlessly.

"Say it," his voice was so harsh it was nearly unrecognizable.

"Dell?" She whimpered praying he'd fulfill her plea as she rubbed herself against his fingers now that he was keeping her from rubbing on his erection.

Instead his hand fisted in the back of her hair and gently pulled her head back until the satiny column of her throat was exposed. The dusky peaks of her nipples jutted forward and Dell inched his hips closer until just the crown of his cock was parting her. His mouth dropped to flick at the tip of one nipple and his deep growl rumbled in his chest and vibrated against her taut nipples.

Chloe gasped and tried to inch her hips forward but Dell's firm hand on her hip kept her in the position he wanted. His mouth opened and he sucked in her breast. The strong tugs of his mouth on her nipple had her moaning and splashing to get him inside her.

His mouth left her nipple, "Say it," he commanded.

"Yes!" Chloe shouted.

His hand on her hip tightened as he slid his cock a few inches deeper. "Yes what?"

Her hips bucked, but he wouldn't relent. "Yes Dell!"

He released her hair and her eyes found his.

"I'm yours," she responded breathlessly, "I accept what we are." She dipped her head to his mouth but his head jerked back.

"And…" he prompted slowly inching closer until her tight pussy slowly spread to accept his rigid girth.

Chloe moaned and bit her lip, her vaginal walls tensing in pleasure at the desired intruder. "I'll do it." Her eyes drifted closed, but Dell roughly grabbed her chin and pulled her head down. Her eyes snapped open to stare at him in shock.

"Do what?" his voice left him on a harsh snarl.

Her shock dissipated when she realized he wanted her submission. She blinked once. "I'll marry you Dell. I'm yours, all yours."

He threw back his head and growled loudly as his hands lowered to her hips and he pulled her so that he was buried fully inside her in one rapid thrust.

Chloe didn't wait, she couldn't. She ached for him. Her hands found his shoulders as she gripped his hips with both her knees and began riding him. The water sloshed and spilled over the tub but she didn't care.

Dell's hands on her hips began to lift her weight to help her rock faster and she rode him until her sex clamped tightly around him, milking his manhood even as she found her own release and gasped his name.

She felt him shooting his warm seed deep inside her and his hands clamped tightly on her ass as he growled, "MINE!"

Chloe collapsed against his chest and the water lapped at her hips as it slowly settled from the turbulent passion they'd shared. He was still rock hard inside her and she couldn't bring herself to pull free and face him, not after what she'd just promised.

"Dell?"

She felt his body tense.

"Can you promise me that everything's gonna be alright."

Hot tears slid down her cheeks.

He pulled her face from his chest to stare at her. "Yes.

Chloe I swear to you on my life. Everything is going be alright.

Nothing will ever happen to you, and if anyone ever wishes to

harm you they'll have to get through me and my pack to do it. I

love you Chloe. You are mine."

Chapter 28

"It'll be your choice Chloe, one you'll have to make alone."

"But,"

"No," Dell cut her off. "There can be no coercion. There can be no interference. It isn't permitted. You'll have to come to the kind of your own volition or not at all."

"W-will it hurt?"

Dell clenched his jaw. "I wish I could say no. I wish I could promise you that the transition was easy, that it was painless, that you wouldn't regret it." His expression darkened, "I can't tell you any of those things so I won't. What I can promise you is that I'll be there with you through it all."

The full moon was finally upon them. There had been little time for Cindy and Mama to plan the ceremony and the wedding, but they'd been so elated at Dell and Chloe's announcement that they'd recruited the pack and everyone had worked tirelessly to get everything ready in time. Even the un-mated men had been welcomed back to the compound. Now that Chloe wore Dell's scent, his wolf had no doubt that his pack mates understood that she belonged to him.

Chloe smiled without humor, "What if something goes wrong tomorrow, what if it doesn't work on me?"

Dell stared at her, "It'll work Chloe, and there will be pain, so be sure it's what you want. I'll be unable to protect you, no matter how much I'll want to, we'll both be helpless unless..." He turned to frown out the window.

"Unless what?" she prodded.

"Unless I refuse to claim you at all."

She sobered, "You wouldn't do that to me. Not now that I've decided. Would you?"

One strong hand snatched up hers as he brought it to his lips, "I wish I could lie to you and say that I would. But I'm selfish Chloe." He tugged on her arm drawing her closer until he bent to rest his forehead against hers. "I want you too badly to ever consider it."

"Good," she sighed nervously, "I don't want any more surprises." She pulled back to stare up at him, "And I don't think I could take it if you said you didn't want me now."

He clamped a hand at her lower back and smiled down at her, "I want you. I'll always want you. You are mine Chloe. Forever."

Smiling weakly she turned imploring chestnut colored eyes up to his. "Tell me," she demanded.

Knowing what she wanted to hear, he cupped her face and kissed her gently before pulling back, "Everything's gonna be alright Chloe."

She sighed heavily and Dell pulled her into the circle of his arms. "Hey, I'm not just paying you lip service. Everything *is* going to be alright. I swear it." His hold tightened. "I'd die before I ever let anything happen to you. Do you know that?"

She nodded, wrapping her arms around him. She truly believed him, and his vow to protect her was the only thing that kept her from fleeing the compound, the city, hell even the state.

She was in love with him. She hadn't said the words yet but she knew it with every fiber of her being.

Her hold on him tightened. She was terrified of the ceremony, of her first change. He'd explained in explicit detail what would happen, but she still had so many questions. Mostly, she just wanted him to be with her and she was having difficulty accepting the fact that she'd have to enter the ceremony alone. She swallowed hard, unsure whether she had the courage to actually go through with it. She didn't know if she was more terrified of the ceremony or of showing her cowardice by failing to follow through.

***

That night the pack celebrated. A great feast was held and Mama regaled the pack with tales of previous ceremonies. She did note that this was the first time that an Alpha had claimed a non-shifter, and it was obvious that she was looking forward to the ceremony.

Chloe was not. She barely ate or drank and her laughter came out as brittle when she tried to laugh at Mama's stories.

Several pack members inquired into her emotions on the great

event and she simply rattled off some lame response, not really

paying attention to anyone or anything.

Finally after supper Dell stood, "Good night," he pulled

Chloe up with him, "we've a long day to prepare for."

Well wishes and bids of good night were delivered on a

chorus of happy voices, but Chloe could only wave meekly as she

trudged woodenly from the table.

She and Dell weren't even out of the dining hall before he

bent and scooped her up into his arms. "I can walk," she

whispered without looking at him.

"You're not even here," he didn't sound annoyed. "I know

your nervous love." His lips brushed her temple, "You're having

difficulty with what's going to happen, but all you need to do is

one thing."

"What," her voice was too hopeful as her eyes found his.

"Trust in me." He crested the stairs and carried her down

the long hallway to their room. "Would I ever let anything happen

to you?"

She shook her head.

"Would I ever do anything to harm you?"

"No."

"Then trust in me tomorrow Chloe. I will protect you. I *will* help you through your first shift. We all will. We are your pack now."

Though the words were meant to bring comfort, Chloe lost the battle with trepidation as it stole through her leaving her feeling cold and alone.

Chapter 29

Chloe stepped from the house, clamping a hand firmly against her flat belly to quell the butterflies flitting within. Her long flowing white gown was a stark contrast to the dark cloudless sky that hosted thousands of brilliant stars all winking as they watched the ceremony begin. As was promised, there was no one there to meet her.

It's do or die! She drew in a breath and stepped down off the porch onto the gravel path that led deep into the woods. Torches alight with flame dotted the path lighting her way.

Should I be this nervous? When she took her first step, the music began. She scanned the area unsure where the speakers were hidden, but it was too dark. She'd only ever heard the song once before, but had instantly thought it striking. As the melody of Apocolyptica's 'Nothing Else Matters' washed soothingly over her, Chloe told herself that in fact, nothing else mattered.

In typical Chloe fashion, she straightened her shoulders and lifted her head as she set out for her destination. Her appearance didn't give away the fact that she was well and truly terrified.

The gravel barely crunched under her slippered feet as she made her way to the tree line. Once there, she stopped and wrung her hands together. Despite the warmth of the August Montana night she couldn't help but shiver as doubt once again seeped through.

I can't do this! She had to fight from taking a step backward. *Dell.* Just the mere thought of him evoked such warmth and feelings of safety that she couldn't help but take a cautious step forward. He's mine and I am his.

She drew in another long slow breath and exhaled more slowly. *You can do this.* She stared at the dark path that lay ahead of her. The torch light wafted gently in the warm night breeze and the flames flicked forward then back as if summoning her. She took a step, then another and continued on the trail until she could see a large fire blazing brightly in the center of the Blackbird stronghold. As she approached, her feet stuttered to a halt.

They were there, all of them and they were waiting on her. Still on the path, partially hidden by the forest she let her eyes scan the forms that stood arms-width apart to form a large circle in the center of the stronghold. AJ, Pony, Stevie, Cindy, Michael, Briggs, and many others. Some were in human form and others stood in the circle in the glory of their wolf figure. Mama stood in the center and Chloe's heart thundered to a halt when she caught sight of her own mother standing next to Mama.

Panic flared to life. *Will she survive once she loses me too?* She wrung her hands together as she stood struggling to call forth the steely resolve she was so well-known for possessing.

Frantically, her eyes searched the circle but caught no sign of Dell. She needed to see him, to know that he was there, that he'd always be there. When she still couldn't find him, she recalled his words. 'You're not dying Chloe, but being reborn. You'll still be the same person, born of the same mother. You won't be kept from your family, merely welcomed into a much larger one.'

She watched as Briggs bent his head and whispered something to Cindy, then he shifted into a large gray wolf and disappeared into the black forest.

What must have only been minutes felt like an eternity as Chloe considered for the thousandth time the ramifications of what would happen if she ran, if she walked away from the family, from the pack, from Dell. When she thought of giving him up, a heavy weight settled on her chest and made it nearly impossible to breathe. She frowned as she forced her feet forward.

When she stepped into the clearing, no one seemed to notice, but then Mama lifted her arms toward the rotund moon and everyone turned to stare at Chloe. She watched as Mama walked toward the fire, an eagle-wing fan in one hand and the other hand balled into a fist. Whatever she held in her fist, she tossed into the fire and when the wind shifted and blew a slight breeze toward Chloe, she inhaled the unmistakable scent of burning sweet grass and sage.

Chloe didn't take her eyes from Mama as she approached the stronghold. She was afraid that Dell wouldn't be there, that he'd changed his mind, that he didn't want her.

The music continued, and the circle parted as Chloe approached, allowing her access then reformed behind her when she stepped inside and walked confidently toward Mama. Mama's knowing eyes twinkled in the firelight.

When Chloe was close enough, Mama grabbed her hand and then took Bea's and pressed mother's and daughter's palms together. "Your mother's lips were the first to kiss yours when you came into this world. Today, they'll be last in this life as she sends you, with her blessing, on your journey to your new life as a member of our family, a member of our pack, and as mate to our Alpha."

Chloe couldn't stop the tears that sprang forth and as she bent to gently kiss her mother's lips. Bea swiped her daughter's tears away and whispered, "With my blessing baby, always with my blessing."

When Bea stepped back and accepted Cindy's hand at a place in the circle, Chloe was slammed with the weight of what was happening. She sawed in breathes as she tried to control her fear. She would change tonight and be changed forever. Sacrificing her way of life to accept the way of the wolf, and she would do it because she was bound inexplicably to the Alpha of the great Northwest Territory.

As if summoned up by her tumultuous emotions, the wind kicked up and twirled her hair and long flowing gown. She was staring at Mama when Mama's gaze shifted to something over Chloe's shoulder. She turned to find Stevie and Cindy placing a buffalo robe, on the ground next to the roaring bon-fire and in front of the entrance to the sweat lodge that had been erected in the center of the circle.

From behind, Mama took her hand and led her to it. Mama knelt and rubbed a hand through the thick coat of the robe before locking her hand in the fur and pulling it up at the edge. On the underside, where the hide was tanned, intricate designs and symbols marked the robe.

"This marks the days of our kind," Mama nodded, "the winter count of our pack." She held up a small hand, "Come."

Chloe knelt unsure of the protocol.

Mama eased her to a kneeling position in the center of the thick buffalo robe.

"Kneel," Mama commanded.

When Chloe did as asked Mama retrieved her eagle-wing fan and used it to draw smoke from the fire. She brushed the smoke down and over Chloe before she turned to the circle and dipped her head once. At the same time, all pack members that weren't already in wolf form shifted so that the entire circle, with the exception of her mother and Cindy's husband Michael, was now shoulder-to-shoulder wolves.

The wolves stepped closer and closer until there was no space between them and they formed a tight circle around Mama, Chloe, and the sweat lodge.

A flash of movement caught her eye and Chloe locked her gaze on the scruff of gray fur that she could see circling just outside the gathering of wolves. The gray wolf was larger than the others, even larger than Briggs. It circled the gathering four times before Mama, still in human form challenged, "He who would claim this mate, do so now!"

The circle broke and the large gray wolf stepped through. Chloe's eyes found his and relief flooded her when she felt the warmth and serenity that only accompanied Dell's gaze.

Mama crossed to pull open the flap to the sweat lodge and motioned for Chloe to enter.

Chloe looked at Dell and while he couldn't speak to her, his warm eyes conveyed his love. She lifted a hand and smoothed it down his muzzle as he stepped closer to her and rubbed his face against her cheek.

Chloe's fingers trembled in his fur and she whispered, "Dell I'm afraid."

Over his shoulder, Mama lifted her arms toward the moon and shouted, "Mitakuye Oyasin!"

Chloe had heard the words before. The phrase was often spoken by many of the family members in prayer before meals. It meant, 'we are all related'.

To Chloe's astonishment, once the words left her lips, Mama shifted. Why Chloe had ever assumed Mama wasn't a shifter she didn't know and seconds later she didn't care as Mama threw back her head and loosed a glorious and triumphant howl. Before Mama's howl broke, one of the wolves in the circle joined in, then the next, and the next.

More and more wolves loaned their voices to the cacophony of howls and others started over until the frenzied howling grew deafening. Chloe didn't care. She was trying to keep her composure, to fight against her natural instinct to run.

Dell had warned her that struggling against the change would only bring her more pain. She'd resolved to not struggle at all, but talking about shifting and actually doing it were two entirely different things.

He licked her cheek then pulled back to stare at her before nodding and nudging her with his snout.

Turning, Chloe slowly entered the sweat lodge and pulled the flap closed behind her. Outside the wolves continued to howl and unsure what to do, she sat in the center of the empty sweat lodge and pulled her knees into her chest and waited.

The chorus of howls stopped abruptly and she sat a little straighter, straining to hear what was happening. The night was cool with a soft breeze, but inside the sweat lodge was becoming stifling. Chloe pulled at the collar of her gown and suddenly wished she could take it off. The small space continued to grow hotter and Chloe eyed the ground around the edges of the lodge wondering if there was a space for air to get in.

Sweat was beading on her forehead and dotted her nose and she pushed her sleeves up and hiked up her skirt to reveal her bare legs. When the room continued to grow hotter she reached for the door wondering if anyone would notice if she lifted the flap slightly to allow in some cool air.

A growl on the other side had her hand stilling. Then she realized that the heat was part of the change. She reclined back on her heels and stared at the flap dying to lift it. Instead, she lifted her hands and pulled on her dress. She heard material tear as she pulled at the collar and it was so hot that she didn't care.

She'd only meant to open the collar a little to allow in some air but once the material was away from her skin she had to have it all away. Her body was fighting so hard to stay cool that she was rapidly losing the energy to do anything else. The last of her strength was spent on jerking her once beautiful gown over her head until she was lying naked, flat on her back on the floor or the sweat lodge. *No wonder it's called a sweat lodge!* She lifted a hand to fan herself, but it didn't help at all.

Her tongue darted out to wet her parched lips, but there was no moisture to share. *I'm so thirsty!* She was laying thinking about the gallon of purple kool-aid she was going to drink when she got out when a sharp spasm of pain tore through her.

She gasped and clamped a hand to her abdomen hoping it was just her thirst, but seconds later it happened again. It started as jolts of pain shooting through her, but they seemed to grow in intensity and frequency the longer she stayed inside the lodge.

At first she tried to quietly breathe through the pains. *God this must be what contractions feel like!* She rose to her knees to rock back and forth steeling herself against the pain. It didn't help, nothing seemed to.

The recovery time between spasms grew shorter and shorter until she was curled on her side into the tightest ball she could form. Panting, sweat dripped off her face and she moaned in agony trying to keep from embarrassing herself or Dell by screaming. She wished the wolves would start howling again so that it would muffle some of her pain-filled noises.

Finally, there was no break from the spasms as they lengthened into one steady searing pain centered in her torso. She tried to remember Dell's instructions. *Relax Chloe!* she cursed herself, but was unable to keep from tensing against the agonizing pain.

She was breathing so rapidly that she was certain, almost hopeful that she'd pass out. No such luck! The pain intensified and she couldn't stop the scream of pain that was tore from her throat as the throbbing agony seemed to crescendo. She thought she felt a momentary breeze on her back but was too busy trying to keep from dying to give a fuck.

Sawing in another breath to let loose another scream it caught in her throat when hands lifted her head. She looked up and saw Dell kneeling over her. He lifted her head into his lap and smoothed her hair back from her face. He too was naked.

"Shhhh, baby. It's gonna be okay. I know it hurts." Tears welled in his eyes even as her own streaked down her cheeks. "Be strong Chloe, just a little bit longer." He pulled her up into his lap and cradled her rocking her back and forth in his arms. "I'm sorry Chloe! I should have never done this to you." His voice broke when she screamed again, "I'm so fucking sorry!"

Her heart nearly broke at the regret in his voice. He was sorry for what he'd done to her. That he hadn't asked her, that he'd simply taken her. Her body trembled as she fought against another scream, not wanting him to hurt knowing that she was in pain. She couldn't suffer through it for herself, but she would for him. She loved him and she'd do whatever it took to be with him.

"It's almost over," his voice was raw with emotion as he kept his head buried at her throat. "It's almost over."

She felt a searing pain in her right forearm and lifted it to see what had happened. There was nothing she could see, but it felt like her arm was on fire. She shoved at Dell's chest and tried to scramble away from him in a panic, but his solid arms locked around her holding her firmly in place. It was then that she realized he was there to help her. To keep her from running from the sweat lodge and embarrassing herself as she had suspected she would have if he hadn't been there forcing her to stay.

A burning flare of pain exploded on her arm and she arched her back and howled in agony, her teeth ground tightly together to keep from screaming. Then something was happening. Her body was changing, she could feel it. Parts of her were becoming much cooler. It started at her feet and shot up her legs. She lifted her burning arm and stared at it only to discover the three familial bands that the pack carried were now emblazoned on her flesh as well.

She dropped her arm when her body dipped and Dell had to shift her weight to pull her tighter in his grip. Suddenly, the wolves outside howled in unison and when she blinked the pain was gone.

Voices carried to her, but they weren't spoken they were in her head. *"Welcome daughter."* She recognized Mama's voice instantly. Before she could process the words, a flood of welcoming sentiments flooded her brain. *"Welcome sister.*

Welcome Aunty. Welcome friend." She recognized Cindy's voice

and Briggs', but there were also several other voices that she didn't

recognize at all. It took her a moment to realize that the

welcoming words were being conveyed to her through the pack

ties that now bound her to the Blackbird pack.

For long moments she lay in Dell's arms trying to catch her

breath. Finally after long moments he pulled back and smiled

down at her with tears in his eyes. "My Chloe." His eyes traveled

down her frame, "My wolf."

He released her and she rolled to her hands and feet. She

was suddenly aware of at least a dozen scents inside the small

space. Dell's tears, her pain, sweetgrass, sage, smoke, the scent of

several people who'd previously occupied the lodge. She could

smell it all.

Dell slowly stood and crossed to the flap before pulling it

open as he smiled down at her. He seemed so much taller now.

He stepped out of the sweat lodge and motioned for her to follow.

She stepped out into the cool night air, but it wasn't as cool as it had been earlier. In fact it wasn't cool at all. It felt similar to the temperature inside the sweat lodge.

The wolves had stopped howling and stared at her as she exited the lodge. Her eyes found her mothers and she opened her mouth to speak to her but nothing came out.

Beside her Dell touched the top of her head and when she turned to look at him he shifted, dropping down to his wolf form but still towering over her. She stared at him and wanted to ask what had happened, but didn't have to. She saw the answer reflected in the amber liquid of his eyes where she stared into the reflective pools and a small brown wolf stared back.

Startled she backed up a step. Before taking a calming breath and approaching to stare at her reflection in Dell's eyes again. *I'm a wolf! Holy shit...I'M A WOLF!"* She looked at her mother again but Bea simply stood with her hands clamped over her lips crying and nodding in approval.

Chloe let her eyes drift down her frame and was stupefied to be staring at what she knew were her feet and hands but were displayed as four small paws.

Beside her Dell nudged her with his head. She looked up and couldn't control herself. She jumped up and bit his ear. When he growled at her she pulled back and flashed what she thought was a smile but was reflected in his eyes as a showing of many pointed teeth.

Behind her one of the wolves whined and she cast a look over her shoulder before she turned, caught Dell by surprise, and bit him on the shoulder before she bolted for the moon bathed forest.

As she raced away she saw him following and recognized the smile in his eyes. The pack hesitated for only a moment before letting loose and racing with Chloe and Dell through the forest on her first run as a member of their pack...their family.

Chapter 30

Walking hand in hand by the frozen stream, Chloe smiled brightly as the warm sun shone down on her and Dell.

Two months had passed since the wedding and things were slowly settling down into a normal routine. She'd moved into the compound and her mother was delighted that her only daughter had finally found someone to share her life with.

The pack too seemed delighted that their Alpha had finally taken a mate and much to Chloe's trepidation they welcomed her into the family with open arms. She and Cindy had even become extremely close friends. So close in fact that Dell often commented that he wasn't sure he approved of the relationship. It was a comment that both Cindy and Chloe chose to ignore.

"You know," Dell laughed eyeing the stream, "when you were going through the change, Mama told me that you were like a parched creek bed that needed to be filled to become what you were meant to be."

Her smile widened as she peeked up at him, "Is that true?"

"Yes. That's something you'll come to learn is that Mama is quite the word-smith."

Chloe giggled and wrapped an arm around Dell's bicep leaning in to rub her cheek on his thickly coated arm. "Well that's good. Words are very powerful."

"And dangerous," he supplied.

They walked in amiable silence a few moments, their feet crunching in the snow, before Dell stopped and turned her to him. "No more secrets love. Nothing between us ever again. Preferably, that would include clothing as well." He winked at her and pulled her close.

Chloe caught her bottom lip between her even teeth. "Dell?"

He leaned down to kiss her cheek then nuzzle her neck, "Mmm?"

"I have one more secret."

He stilled, before slowly lifting his face to frown at her.

"I," she began then flushed. "Christ, how do I say this?"

"Say it," he demanded.

"I snuck into town last week. I met with someone," she felt his body tensing against hers. "He…"

"He?" His teeth were clamped together and the word came out on a growl.

"I needed his help. I was having problems, and I couldn't go to you."

Dell frowned down at her. "You sought out another male rather than coming to me?"

She shook her head vigorously, "It wasn't like that Dell I just needed his…"

"His what?" Dell demanded harshly, his eyes darkening dangerously. "Did he touch you?"

Chloe backed up a step, "Yes, but…"

Dell threw back his head and growled ferociously.

Chloe backed up further, "Dell stop! You're being an idiot!"

He dropped his head and stalked her, "*Where* did he touch you?"

Her cheeks flamed and at the telling sign Dell lunged. He caught her around the waist and yanked her into him as one hand gently fisted her hair. "You let him touch you intimately," he accused on a snarl.

Her cheeks bright with indignation, Chloe relaxed in his hold. "Yes. *He's* my doctor."

Suddenly, Dell's angry sneer disappeared. His nostrils flared and he inhaled deeply, his brows furrowing in concern, "Are you well?"

"No," shoving at his chest until he released her she stalked a few paces from him before she turned and lifted her chin, "I took a pregnancy test Dell."

His mouth fell open and his eyes grew wide. He was frozen for several long moments before his lips slowly curled into a wide smile. "Pregnant?" He rushed to her and lifted her into his arms, spinning in a tight circle. "We're going to have a baby?" He pressed his lips to hers and pulled back to yell, "WE'RE GOING TO HAVE A BABY!"

"Dell!"

He dropped his delighted eyes to hers.

"We are *not* having a baby."

Trepidation stole over him only to be quickly replaced by fear. "We're…"

A brilliant smile split Chloe's features as she lifted her arms and wrapped them around his neck, her lips found his and instead of kissing him she whispered against his mouth, "We're having two."

Skin Walkers: Conn
by
Susan A. Bliler

Aries kept her head down as she was led down the long

narrow corridor. She rubbed at her arms in an attempt to ward off

the chill that had crept over her when she'd envisioned the damp

cold cell she anticipated being kept in.

Conn pulled her to a halt and grabbed the front of his shirt,

ripping it open and sending buttons bouncing on the linoleum

floor. He pulled his arms free and wrapped the shirt around Aries'

shoulders. "Sorry if it smells bad."

It still held warmth from his body and Aries pulled it

tighter around herself, whispering a "thank you" before noticing

the earthy, spicy scent she now knew to be his. She inhaled deeply

finding an odd comfort in the scent even as her eyes slid to stare at

the form fitting white under shirt that clung to his chiseled torso

like a second skin.

His arms were huge, bulging with thickly corded muscle.

The deep tan of his skin only added emphasis to the stark contours.

Several scars resembling claw marks marred one rounded shoulder. Aries wondered if the same creature was the one to leave the long scar down his face as well. She liked the scar on his face it made him seem fierce. *Hell, he'd seem fierce without it.*

She was led out double swinging doors as they entered what appeared to be a fancy hotel lobby before she was steered to a glass elevator. Conn followed her in, his hand still clamped—not roughly—on her arm.

As they rode up, Aries lifted her head to stare at the beautiful manor and out the large picture windows that dotted the front of the building. It was night time, dark outside, and the lights were low and dim inside. In the night she could just make out thick fluffy flakes as they drifted gently to the earth. She sucked in a sharp breath.

It'd been six years since she'd last seen snow, and she'd missed it more than she ever could have imagined. The sharp sting of tears at her eyes had her lifting a hand and placing it on the glass of the elevator. She could almost feel the snow in her hand. She didn't know that Conn watched her curiously.

The elevator went up to the third floor and stopped before the doors slid open. They exited onto a beautiful navy carpet with gold designs that covered the expanse of the third floor. The hall was long with dark oak doors alternating on either side of the hall. Again she couldn't help but feel that the estate felt more like a luxury resort than the hide-out for Walkers....*whatever in the hell a Walker is!*

At the end of the hall Conn pulled a key card from his pocket and scanned it quickly on the security sensor. The door didn't beep, simply clicked open.

Conn placed a hand on Aries' shoulder to keep her from entering. He strode past her and inspected the room before turning to her, "It's clear."

Outside the door, Aries balked. Her mind was going a mile-a-minute. She'd seen a grandiose staircase in the center of the building. Her eyes flicked to the door knob. If she jerked the door closed, it might just buy her enough time to make it to the stairs. *But it's fucking freezing outside. Even if I did escape, I'd die of exposure.*

The corner of Conn's mouth lifted, "You might make it to the second floor, but that'd be it. The manor houses many Walkers, and at least one of *my* men is quartered on each floor."

When Aries didn't move Conn's smile disappeared, "Not to mention that the drugs are still in your system and you haven't eaten. Your too weak Aries, don't try it."

He was right, but it didn't keep her from lifting her chin defiantly and contemplating slamming the door in his face just to piss him off.

Dissatisfied with her lack of movement Conn dropped his head to eye her, the lines of his body now taut with challenge, "You have two seconds to get your ass in this room."

Aries' voice was soft, "And if I don't."

Conn did something than that surprised and shocked her. His typically angry features broke into a heart stopping smile, revealing perfect white teeth and an air of youth that made him, for once, seem not so harsh, but his next words dispelled any hope. His challenge was simple. "Find out."

Aries pulled his oversized shirt tighter around her before stepping into the room.

Conn locked the door behind her before crossing the room and drawing the blinds closed. The suite was elegant. Dimly lit lamps dotted the main sitting room and a small chandelier hung over a cherry wood table to her left in the small dining and kitchen area.

Conn pointed down the only hall in the suite. "Bathroom's at the end of the hall and your room is on the right. There should be clothes on the bed. I suggest you shower while I prepare dinner."

Aries' teeth caught her bottom lip. "I thought I was going to the holding cells?"

Conn frowned down at her, "How do you know about the holding cells?"

She dropped her eyes, "You mentioned them in the car."

Conn snorted before crossing into the kitchen and turning on the faucet to wash his hands, "Aries, I'm tired, I'm starving, and

I'm cranky. I suggest you get in the shower before I decide to give you one myself."

Her brows drew together as she frowned at his back.

He turned then, "Did I forget to mention that I'm horny?"

Aries felt her cheeks flame and she turned to quickly walk down the hall. She heard Conn laughing at her quick retreat.

Down the hall she flicked on a light in what Conn had deemed to be her room to discover an interior as exquisite as any she'd ever seen. A large canopied bed sat against one wall while large cherry wood furnishings adorned the room. The muted tan and soft yellow of the drapes and carpet, were also reflected in the satiny bed spread and array of pillows on the bed, giving the room a warm homey feel. A fire blazed in a hearth across from the bed and next to the sole window in the room.

Aries crossed to the window and peered out. She found the mechanism to roll the window open and quickly did so before popping the screen out. She was leaning halfway out the window when she jumped at Conn's voice.

"There's no way down."

Aries pulled back into the room sheepishly, "I know... I wasn't..." She held up her hand and it was full of already melting snow. "I just wanted to touch it."

About the Author

Susan Bliler, a Legal Services Investigator for the State of Montana, has been writing since college.

She is a graduate of the University of Great Falls, where she earned her Bachelor's Degree in Paralegal Studies and minored in Criminal Justice.

She lives in Great Falls, Montana with her husband and two dogs (labs).

Susan is currently at work on her new series, Skin Walkers.

Visit her at SusanBliler.com for exclusive excerpts of soon to be released works.

Made in the USA
Middletown, DE
08 December 2017